Also by Stephen J. Lyons

Landscape of the Heart
A View from the Inland Northwest
The 1,000-Year Flood
Going Driftless
West of East

Searching for A Way Home

Misadventures with Misanthropes

essays by

Stephen J. Lyons

Finishing Line Press
Georgetown, Kentucky

Searching for A Way Home

Misadventures with Misanthropes

For Jan

ACKNOWLEDGMENTS

- Northern Idaho without A Clue: *The Forge Literary Magazine*
- North to Alaska: *The Satirist*
- How I Failed at Farming: *Chicago Reader*
- Elvis Imitators on Spring Break: *The Sun*
- My Extra Year: *Adbusters*
- Under the Influence: *The Sun*
- Young Chicago Boy Talks to God: *Longridge Review* (Nominated for a Pushcart Prize in 2020.)

Publisher: Leah Huete de Maines
Editor: Christen Kincaid
Cover Art: Provided by the author
Author Photo: Provided by the author
Cover Design: Elizabeth Maines McCleavy

Order online: www.finishinglinepress.com
also available on amazon.com

Author inquiries and mail orders:
Finishing Line Press
P. O. Box 1626
Georgetown, Kentucky 40324
U. S. A.

Table of Contents

"You never know where life will take you."
—My Permanent Liminal Space

Sex and the Single Cowboy

The very first time I met AJ Gorbett I nearly got punched out. The A was for Allen, the J was thrown in. All I was doing was coming up behind him in my usual non-intrusive, non-competitive, quiet, early 1970s way to introduce myself as the chief cook and bottle washer for the Colorado outfit called the Diamond Arrow Dude Ranch. AJ was the wrangler, just in from the Lubbock Stockyards and full of all this bullshit Texas cowboy etiquette. Like, don't swear in front of a guy's girlfriend; never drink less than twenty cups of black coffee a day; and, for God sakes, don't, under any circumstances, sneak up behind a cowpoke. You'll liable to get decked.

After all, these western types are wired on Copenhagen, one-night stands, and green colts, like the two-year-old Mayjoe AJ bought for $200 down on the Navajo reservation: just as wild as any horse would be after a few miserable winters pawing among the rabbitbrush around dumps like Tuba City and Kayanta, where the red rock cliffs are overshadowed by the orange glow from Howard Johnson's.

At least that's the cowboy myth and no one believed that crap more than AJ Gorbett. In fact, he thrived on the cowboy image. A regular Marlboro Man. Whenever an attractive-looking woman stayed at the Diamond, it was always, "Yes, ma'am, no ma'am." "Cowboying is lonesome, but a man's gotta do what he's gotta do." Then he'd take his black Stetson off, real gentlemanly like, while the poor woman (a Methodist just up from the asphalt ranges of Houston) fell in love with him. I saw it happen a dozen times that summer.

Dammit, he *was* handsome. Tall, and dark of course, with a slight limp that seemed more than than slight when talking to the ladies. From the rodeo he'd say, suddenly full of awkward shyness with a look across his mug that indicated he didn't want to talk about it. Too painful. But he'd go on and talk about it anyway; busting bulls on the B-grade circuit in eastern Oregon, Idaho, and Texas; and breaking broncs the Apache way by leading horses out into deep creeks and then jumping on bareback.

And me just standing there fading into the background like a coat rack, hating his cowboy guts, his Texas accent, the way he held his coffee cup and cigarette with the same hand. Knowing that the rodeo limp came when he fell out of my truck cold-drunk, standing to pee while we were rounding a corner coming back from a grain run.

And knowing when night came, AJ would be rolling in the arms of that same attractive woman (by now a *lapsed* Methodist) with his hat on the bedpost and, if he really felt sensitive that night, he'd take his boots off. I'd once again retire alone to my tent, pet my blue heeler, Emmie, and fall asleep listening to the whirl of the Coleman lantern while reading Hermann Hesse. It was a long, lonely western summer.

In the morning I'd have to face him, in fact have to serve him his fucking eggs and coffee while he grinned at me and went into precise, editorial detail about his night of carnal gymnastics; this position and that position, and something called the "heifer delight," involving lariats and spurs.

There was no more of the polite "yes, ma'am, no ma'am, cowboying is the only life where a man is truly free" AJ. No, it was "God, what a tight ass. You should see her without her clothes. She wouldn't stop screaming."

Then, after showing me the alleged bites and scratches, he'd start to rub it in a bit. "Did you rope your mule last night? You know you're only supposed to rope your mule if he comes up. It's bad luck to rope your mule if he doesn't come up." Why didn't I pour hot grease down his faded Wrangler shirt with the extra-long tails?

AJ's dog was worse. One Way is what he called him. "One Way and Hell-bent for leather!" AJ boasted. A regular cur if you want to know the truth. One of those dogs running around the West people claim are "part-wolf." Right and I'm part Cherokee.

Whenever Emmie came within eyeshot of One Way, AJ would yell, "Kill Emmie, One Way. Kill her! And damned if that sorry pot-licker wouldn't charge Emmie (who was only about a year old, recovering from kennel cough, and not nearly as smart as the heeler Wade the plumber owned, who would fetch metric sockets, right size and all out of the pickup and cart them to him under the bunkhouse), grab her around the neck and make menacing growls until AJ, who never got tired of this joke, would finally tell One Way to stop.

I swear Emmie's never recovered. Sometimes when I feel nostalgic, I'll whisper One Way's name to Emmie, now 12 and incontinent, and her ears will perk up, then she'll bury her head in my lap whimpering.

But I'm getting off track here. This story is about AJ Gorbett, Mister Western Cowboy Himself, and all the cruelty he leveled my way and all the acrobatic sex he somehow finagled out in the middle of nowhere Colorado, while I was stuck with "Magister Ludi and the Bead Game" and, yes, a summer of roping my mule whether it came up or not.

One Friday night AJ took me with him to Durango to teach me how to pick up women. Felt sorry for me he said, living a life of celibacy in a tent, eating raisins and nuts. "I'm worried you'll go blind, Lyons," is how he delicately put it. I'll admit my eyesight is bad.

Bell bottoms and sandals would never cut it, according to the expert, and might provoke a brawl at this particular bar, where weekend patrons still flew through the plate glass windows startling the tourists walking by. So AJ dressed me in tight Wranglers, boots, and a paisley shirt, topped with a beige hat with porcupine quills in the brim (from a road kill). There was nothing AJ could do about the wire-rim glasses and my Liberal smirk.

I must say I looked good. Even One Way cocked his empty head my way, and didn't register his usual growl when I stepped over him. The ZZ Top blaring in AJ's pick-em-up truck sounded richer than just three chords and maybe, just maybe, I thought, I might have some cowboy blood running through my Chicago veins. After all, I did grow up "behind the yards." The Texas drawl could come later and anyone can bust broncs and fake a limp.

At the Stockyard Bar after a few beers, AJ poked me and said, "She's looking at you. Tip your hat to her. she might be a barrel racer and you know what that means. Ask her to dance." It was difficult to assess the situation as rapidly as AJ could, and I had no idea what sexual repertoire a barrel racer had, but for some vague reason I trusted his judgment and besides, he did this every Friday night with disgusting success and I had just finished my last Hesse book, so I sauntered over as best as I could wearing Tony Lamas that were two sizes too large. Events then moved rapidly and it was to be the last time I saw AJ that weekend. The barrel racer actually had a glass eye that wandered so it was hard to tell just who she was looking at. After we danced a couple of awkward western numbers, she ditched me for a biker. I ended up in a Main Street alley with the dry heaves.

Cowboys, bikers. What's the difference? I walked the 12 miles home to the ranch cursing AJ and each boot-induced blister along the way. Next day I quit the mass cooking profession and went back to college where pursued a seven-year undergraduate degree.

AJ, last I heard, was a collections agent on the Navajo reservation working for a shadowy car firm out of Snowflake, Arizona. A just reward if you ask me. And every Christmas I get a postcard from him with the following message: "Lyons, did you rope your mule last night? You know you're only supposed to rope your mule . . ."

Slacking at the Elliot Hotel

In the lobby of the ancient Elliot Hotel in Astoria, Oregon, the old man was eating cold hot dogs right out of the package on stale buns. No condiments.

Want one?" he said, offering me the bag.

"Sure, why not."

I was always hungry back then. The 1979 World Series was airing on a black-and-white television. I favored the Orioles over the Pirates because I loved birds, but truthfully I had wandered into the hotel to escape the persistent coastal rain.

My dinner companion was one of the many old men who lived in the hotel, a place that served as a final waystation for widowers, aged sea salts, and raggedy strays whose meager social security checks afforded them a warm room and a hot plate for a fair price. They had chased salmon up and down the Columbia River. They had cut down trees in the great forests of the Pacific Northwest. Their bodies were worn out. Their working years were spent in an era when fish and trees were plentiful. Now that era and their lives were coming to an end.

I felt at home at the hotel, and began to spend my evenings there, probably because the way my life was going it was not a stretch to imagine my future reflected in the grizzled faces of these men.

I was 23-year-old college dropout with a job title that could be best described as "laborer." At the time I had lied myself on to a tree planting job across the Columbia River in Washington state. During the interview the foreman asked if I had any experience using something called a "hoedad." I had no earthly idea what a hoedad was, but of course I said I had used one for years "down in California." Turned out it was an ax-like tool that you dig into the ground, lift up the soil and drop a tiny tree plug in the hole.

I became all too familiar with hoedads as I climbed up and down steep, slick, ankle-twisting hillsides planting six-inch nursery-grown trees every nine-feet for twelve hours a day. It was classic migrant piece work and if I made $20 it was a good day. After three weeks of working in the rain and developing a persistent cough I simply ignored the alarm clock one morning. No one called to check up on me. I was not missed.

The country was more forgiving of slackers back then. My "gap year" between college enrollments turned into a half decade of lousy jobs and unpaid bills. Like so many of us in the 1970s, I was firmly committed to "fighting the Man." Corporate America was evil, corrupting, and soul deadening. I wanted no part of succumbing to it.

The problem was I did not know exactly what I wanted. But I did foolishly believe I was *different*, artistic even, and that I would not bend to the will of a 9-5 job.

At that time, the economy up and down the coast was in free fall. In Astoria, the Bumble Bee cannery—a major employer in town—was about to move south to San Diego. Unemployment hit double figures. And it never stopped raining.

For entertainment I would walk down to the docks and watch the cranes load up our old growth trees to send across the Pacific in freighters only to return on those same ships as milled boards to sell in American lumber yards. Meanwhile, our own lumber yards were closing down. Millworkers were laid off. Nothing made sense.

I worked for a roofing company (also named Bumble Bee) for three days until I was fired for being too slow. I hauled sheetrock for a deranged carpenter on speed at a construction site until I quit or was sacked at exactly the same time. Who could tell?

I tried out to be a firefighter. I did well on the written exam, but failed the physical part of the test where I could not lift and carry a hose up a ladder to a second-story window. A mink farm was hiring, but when the boss explained to me that my job required killing those cute creatures by pithing their spinal columns I said, "no thanks."

The few occasions when I could splurge, I treated myself to a steam bath, a popular hangout for stinky fishermen and dock workers. For a few bucks and a smuggled beer I could sweat the disappointments of the day away and pretend that, when I emerged after an hour, clean, shiny and mildly intoxicated, that my prospects would have improved.

But I was only fooling myself. Eventually I would have to go back to college, get that degree, and join the millions of other Boomers that would have no choice but to bend to the will of capitalism.

Yet, I admit, foolishly nostalgic as the years fly by, that I miss the struggle. I dearly miss the former bare-knuckled fight in me, the idealistic young man who pushed against the tide, who swam upstream against the current and whose path was hardly straight.

And I miss those guys at the Elliot Hotel, who generously took me in: no questions asked. As if I belonged. As if I needed warmth and food. As if there was still plenty for all of us.

Northern Idaho without A Clue

Desiccated chicken legs under the chairs. Piles of twisted accordion-shaped Budweiser tall boys. Coffee can of shotgun shells. Stray Cheerios float atop milk drops on a vinyl tabletop. Cat scratch couch arm with exploded stuffing. Television on, volume off, Spokane station, a blur of staticky snow. Two teenage boys devour a sack of Cheetos, their fingers stained a color not found in nature. Early 1980s in rural northern Idaho.

Lou Fielder has taken me under his wing. I'm sitting in his living room where everyone smokes and no one aspires to be lean. My temporary home is down the gravel road in a drafty rental with a faulty chimney that will eventually catch fire when I'm on the other side of the valley, steam cleaning machinery for a local farmer. His wife will open the back door and calmly call out, *Your house is on fire*. The only words she will ever speak to me. A week later Idaho will experience its biggest earthquake ever, a 6.9 ground shudder. Downstate, new valleys will cleave and open in a geological instant. But by then everything I owned was in the farmer's unheated, mouse-infested trailer, and I was trying to work off my debt to him before the first snow.

But that's weeks away. On this bright autumn afternoon, Lou fills a dented Stanley thermos with boiling coffee and we load up into his green, four-wheel drive Dodge Power Wagon, circa 1970 something, with a winch on the front of a deer-repelling bumper. I do not believe it has ever been washed. Forget seatbelts. They are seen as a government plot. We set off to do what we do every day: drive back roads, drink coffee, spot moose, and cut wood. Under Lou's tutelage, I learn that the best wood is red pine and tamarack. Burns slowly and evenly. Leave the aspen. Burns like paper.

I'm in my late twenties, broke, in limbo, waiting for my life to kick start. I've got nothing going for me. A year earlier, after hearing Bob Dylan's "Blood on the Tracks" album, I dropped out of college in search of blue collar credibility. I thought writing in my journal qualified me as a talented artist. Someone with special insights. I spent many hours in coffee shops. I read too much Hesse and Castaneda. I consciously inserted the word *muse* into conversations, opting for the upper case version, such as "The Muse is especially strong tonight." I tell people I'm between jobs, but that's a lie. I'm between lives.

I drifted to Idaho because someone once told me that that Idaho is what America was. I also liked the way Idaho looked on a map. There were all these blank places without roads.

Except for a month on a Ford assembly line in Detroit that Lou doesn't like to discuss, he has lived in northern Idaho all his life. He survives on poaching, huckleberry picking, dumpster diving, and shadowy jobs that involve midnight drives down to Boise. His quarter section of land belonged to his great grandfather who died of the 1918 Influenza. His headstone is visible out Lou's kitchen window. All of Lou's deceased relatives are buried behind the house. In Idaho you can do things like that—bury your kin in your backyard.

We're an odd couple but somehow it works. Best thing is that when Lou talks I don't have to say anything. He doesn't ask me if I have a plan for the foreseeable future, and I don't ask him about the out of season elk steaks in his freezer. Besides, he tells the best stories. Some of them are made up but I don't care. Too much is made about whether something is fact or fiction, truth or tale. A good story doesn't have to be true. It just has to be told right.

"You know how I lost this?" Lou asks, holding up his right hand with the index finger missing, as we head out on Spring Valley Road. "Was fishing on the Snake for steelhead but hooked onto one of them slimy sturgeon that sit on the bottom in the river silt. Must of been seven feet long and a hundred years old. Pulled him up on the beach, tried to take the hook out, and the goddamned pot licker chomped my pointer off. Clear through the bone. Bite was so clean it hardly bled. Then he flopped back in the water. But, before he took off, he turned around and, I kid you not, he winked at me." He uses the phrase *goddamned pot licker* often and it refers to any creature that might bite your finger off.

"Now pour me some of that mud." I open the thermos. The Folger's instant is still bubbling. We are bouncing around on Idaho's infamous washboard roads, so I try not to spill the coffee on my crotch.

Northern Idaho is Appalachia West but more isolated. Shocking poverty contrasted by the most lovely forests and hills. Canyons that only see two hours of natural light a day. The most endangered wildlife hunted relentlessly. Muddy pickups in various states of broken scattered across front yards: valet parking for the poor. Everyone is armed—locked and loaded and twitchy fingered. Snarling wolf-hybrid dogs covered with fat ticks loll in the yards like lions waiting for their chance to pounce. Children with bad teeth stare slowly at cars passing through town. The worst kids throw rocks, but only at vehicles with out-of-town license plates. A favorite bumper sticker: "Welcome to Idaho. Now go home!" Perilous two-lane highways barely wide enough to contain logging trucks that carry out the last of the old growth without ceremony. The weather is always cloudy with a chance of fire.

Lou says we need to pay a visit to Virgil Small, the horse logger. Last month someone poisoned his team of Belgians. Splashed acid in their eyes. For vengeance. Probably his neighbor, Lou says. That's one story. Another story making the rounds is that the horses have gone blind because of bad nutrition.

Some essential mineral lacking in their diet, like potassium or selenium. Lou isn't sure which story is true and, like me, he doesn't really care.

"Hey," Lou says, as we pass a wood chip truck, its cargo flying out the back like wooden snowflakes and forcing Lou to turn on the wipers. "What's Idaho foreplay?" He won't answer until I repeat his question. It's extremely irritating.

"OK. I give up, Lou. What's Idaho foreplay?"

"You awake?"

Virgil is seventy, short and squinty with thick, black nerd glasses. On his head sits a steel helmet of the kind loggers wear. As if it could protect you from a falling ponderosa pine. As if you'd want to survive a head shot from a widow maker. He wears bibbed overalls over a dirty long-sleeved shirt. Thermal undershirt underneath. Snub-nosed pencil and a small notebook stick out of the front pocket. Muddy boots. I shake sandpaper hands. Mine are as soft as velour. He talks to me as if I am some kind of official investigator of animal abuse, not an itinerant laborer wannabe artist without two nickels to rub together.

I spot the pair of blonde Belgians. They float through the trees like ghosts, magnificent in their freakish size. Virgil passes his palm quickly over the two horses' eyes to prove they can't see. "Look, they don't even blink." Virgil moves confidently between the team, swatting away knuckle-sized horse flies, patting their hams, stroking their noses. "Just look there, Steve. That's all horse there, yes sir. That's all horse."

He rattles off the names of past logging camps: Enterprise. Sandpoint. Priest Lake. Kalispell. All tourist towns now. Places of soft hands filled with people like me—without a clue. Virgil says despite the blindness he'll still take his horses into the woods this winter. Says his team can work by instinct.

Virgil's wife Evelyn sells Fuller brushes. Talks about God and leaves pastel-colored religious tracts in post offices throughout northern Idaho. She's thin as a whisper in men's dungarees, a red-plaid wool shirt, worn boots. Despite the work clothes she appears feminine, bird-like, someone who notices everything.

Virgil and Evelyn's trailer leans off kilter in a patch of sickly pines. No electricity or water. They pay a deacon at church fifty bucks a month to park their trailer on his land.

"My neighbor over there. I'm sure it's him that done it." Virgil points and I look up a scabby hill toward another trailer, this one surrounded by a barbed wire fence and a locked gate with a no trespassing sign posted. Four-wheel truck with a gun rack sits in front. A half dozen chained mongrels scratch in the dirt, itching for a fight.

"Horses got loose one night during a storm. Made a mess of his garden. Well, he come down here with his shorts all in a bunch and says 'Get your god damned horses off my land. If I wanted neighbors I would of lived in town!' Two days later my horses were blind. I know he done it. I just know it."

Virgil won't report the incident to the sheriff because like most Idahoans he doesn't trust any branch of law enforcement, Feds most of all. "Evie says 'God will take care of him.'" In due time, he adds.

Dusk arrives. Evelyn lights a Coleman lantern, takes up knitting needles, and hums "The Old Rugged Cross." We sit propped up in lopsided lawn chairs huddled against the crisp air around a table made from one of those huge round wooden disks the power company wraps cable around.

The coffee catches up with me and I need to use the bathroom. Virgil leads the way into the dark trailer where he hands me a Planter's peanut can and points toward the back where there once was a functional toilet, now covered with boxes of Fuller products. He waits outside the thin sliding door muttering. Because of his presence and the clumsiness of holding the can, it takes me forever to get my stream started. When I finally emerge I hand him the container of warm piss and he disappears outside.

I look around the trailer and realize that except for the horses, Virgil and Evelyn have nothing of material substance. In that way we are alike, but they seem happier. More settled with their situation, as desperate as it seems. Stacks of yellowed newspapers. Curry combs. Dirty dishes. Burnt orange afghan throws. Flaky linoleum. A hole in the wall. Useless lighting and plumbing fixtures. Water jugs. Mouse traps. Dusty curtains with scenes of cowboys roping steers. Copies of *Scenic Idaho*, circa 1950s, thirty-five cents. "Exploring Idaho's Mystery Land, The Big Horn Crags." "Colter's Hell: A Historical Story." "Complexities of Law Enforcement at Ft. Hall." At the end of the hallway a bed made up neatly with flowered pillows and a log cabin quilt. Above the bed a wooden cross.

Back outside Lou is retelling his missing finger story to Evelyn, who is now humming "What A Friend We Have in Jesus," almost in synch with the clicking of her knitting needles. The culprit is now a pet badger that turned rogue on Lou. This time the badger smiles with the finger dangling from the side of his mouth "like a cigarette, 'cept it was my pointer pointin' at me! Never saw the goddamned pot licker again. And I raised him from a baby." The word *goddamned* elicits a look of reproach from Evelyn, but I'm not sure Lou notices.

I hear the Belgians shuffling in their enclosure. Virgil starts talking about the past, how he's been chasing the old growth across the Northwest for fifty years. How at first it seemed endless, a dark green sea grove from horizon to horizon, impenetrable rain forests of bough and rafter. Wet trees of two hundred rings. Trees where a dozen men holding hands could not complete a circle around the base. Logging trucks with one tree per load. Trees with the truest grain. Douglas-fir. Port Orford cedar. Humboldt redwood.

The same land now a replanted monoculture of fast growing hemlock factory trees that are harvested in only twenty years. Harder for the little guys to find work, the gypsy loggers, the *gyppos*. Mills closing up and down the Pacific Coast.

"If you don't believe me, go down to the docks over there in Astoria and watch our raw logs head to China and Japan, and then come back a month later and watch the same boats come back and unload finished boards. Makes no earthly sense." When she hears the word *earthly* Evelyn closes her eyes and smiles. She doesn't believe in the concept of earthly.

Most folks up here blame the enviros—the Earth First hippies and the tree spikers—but Virgil says it was human greed that led to this. Shakes his head and says, "I never thought we'd run out of trees. No sir. Never thought…" Evelyn stops her humming and knitting, looks over at Virgil and reminds him that "God will provide. He always has and He always will. We'll get through."

Virgil keeps talking. Darkness finally hides his face until all you see is his metal helmet bobbing like a rabbi in prayer.

A yard light goes on in front of the neighbor's trailer spotlighting our circle. I see a barrel of a man stagger out the doorway carrying a bag of dog food. Like many men in northern Idaho he wears a holster and a sidearm. Assume it's loaded, safety off. When they see him, the dogs bark and howl like a pack of wolves, and jump on him as if he is prey. He swears, kicks them off roughly, and pours kibble into two dingy plastic buckets. They devour the grub and then begin to growl and fight over the buckets. The neighbor ignores them, looks over at our small circle, takes out his gun, points it in our direction, and yells.

His actions shatter the mellow fellowship of Evelyn's hymns, Virgil's stories, Lou's jokes, and the serenity of the crisp Idaho evening. The neighbor's rage takes over. He rants about the horses, the stink, the flies they attract, their "shit piles," the damage to his land; the "damn government" with its black helicopters spying on him. That part about the black helicopters was a frequent gripe back then and was discussed in most rural cafes by both the sober and the intoxicated.

I think back to a similar incident six years earlier when an old cowboy in Colorado took a shot at me. He was crouched with his rifle behind a pickup truck, his girlfriend next to him, her beehive hairdo peeking up like a periscope above the bed's frame. They were both beyond drunk. Turned out he was shooting at my blue heeler Emmie Lou, not at me. At first I was enraged and began to charge toward at him, but then I came to my senses, grabbed Emmie, and got the hell out of there. Ran into the guy the next day and he was as friendly as ever. There is nothing more erasable than a drunk's memory.

Without a word, Lou disappears back to the Power Wagon, where I know he keeps a loaded Israeli made, Desert Eagle .50 caliber handgun in the glove box along with a box of ammo. "My goddamned potlicker stopper," be once told me, fondling it tenderly.

As I nervously watch Virgil's neighbor stomp around waving his weapon, it occurs to me that I have not made much progress since my last run in with an angry western gunslinger. What am I doing here? What's next? Shouldn't I be further along in my life? Past the stage where I am pissing in a coffee can while on the verge of becoming a gunshot victim? Beyond these idle months of driving around gazing at scenery and waiting for something, *anything*, to happen?

But this evening it occurs to me that the life I've been waiting for has been here all along. So this is it! An evening in the Idaho woods, surrounded by the warmth of fellowship *and* the threat of bodily harm. The entire human condition revealed. How had I missed this before? Looking back today, I felt at that moment as if I had just come out of an unconscious state. Maybe it was one of those *your life flashes before you* moments before you die. Except, I wanted to live.

"Ah, don't pay him no attention," Virgil says to me. "He does this most nights. We're used to his shenanigans."

But something tells me this is a not a normal night. I spot Lou quietly circling around the woods toward the neighbor, crouching like he's in special ops. I see something silver in his right hand, the one with the missing finger. The Belgians whinny and stamp. Virgil calls to them. "Easy guys, easy now." The neighbor's dogs growl. Evelyn continues to knit calmly, then softly hums "Count Your Blessings," a hymn I recognize from church camp. I begin to hum with her. She stops her handiwork, looks up, smiles gratefully, and nods to me. Together we sing:

> *So, amid the conflict whether great or small,*
> *Do not be disheartened, God is over all;*
> *Count your many blessings, angels will attend,*
> *Help and comfort give you to your journey's end.*

Fear and Loathing in Alaska: Where Men Are Men and The Bears Are Pretty Scary

Snow is falling, but I am not in a white world. At the Anchorage airport, broad-faced natives move through the lobby with the weary look of the world's indigenous; Pacific-rim Asians with deal-making cell phones dial home; and an African running a shoe-shine booth polishes another pair of Rockports. Sled dogs in animal carriers howl like wolves caught in snares, their pleas echo through the concourse and outdoors into the Chugach Mountains. Outside, whatever light gets through the heavy cloud cover looks sallow. It's the end of March, but the feeling more closely resembles a non-ending February, somewhere at the jumping off point at the north end of the earth—the edge of what's known. Where I'm going is another plane ride away on Kodiak Island, where there are 3,000 brown bears and around 10,000 humans.

Hazel, an airport travel assistant, unfolds a map of this giant state and warns me, "Watch out for the bears on Kodiak. They're awake you know." I tease her. "What if I find a cute cub? Can I pick him up?"

She doesn't think I'm funny. "Only if you want to end up in the obituaries of the newspaper."

I have traveled to Alaska to profile an emergency room doctor on Kodiak Island. Here in Anchorage I'm four time zones from Wall Street, 1,500 miles away from Seattle, as far north as Helsinki, and as far west as Honolulu. Out there in the bush are the sleds and the mushers and the mail planes that drop from the sky to land on permafrost and ocean surf. Alaska is water, glaciers, mountains, muskeg and, every second, ice melting beneath a warming planet.

In the dimly lit, lower level of the airport are glass cases of stuffed trumpeter swans, dall sheep, and brown bear, sterile remnants of Alaska's bounty. That bounty may be endless in reputation, but cod fishermen come back with less and less each year; loggers strip entire islands of old growth trees; Alaska's killing fields of trappers and trophy hunters are legendary. And there's still so much more, at least for the next few quick decades. This is our Outback, our own private Amazon—the last wild place we can act out our antiquated Robinson Crusoe wilderness fantasies, or escape from ex-wives, child support, and other tragedies that occur Down Below.

Only six hundred thousand people live up here and after two years of residency every man, woman, and baby receives a check from the Alaska Permanent Fund, their share of the Alaska's oil profits. This particular year that amounts to $1,606.

Near the PenAir ticket counter, dialects drift in and out like steam in a dream. Native girls giggle and line up for Starbuck's mochas. The clerk might be from a village in Nepal or Tibet. She might be Hindu or Muslim, and once wore a sari, but now she is dressed in a crisp Starbuck's apron. She jockeys an espresso machine like a veteran and asks us the most important question of the moment. "Do you want two percent, soy, or whole milk?"

A native woman in mukluks strides past in a full-length sealskin coat with fur trim. At the BP ticket counter, several dozen rough-looking oil workers with duffel bags and dirty Carthart sweatshirts wait in line for their ticket packets for the flight up to Deadhorse at Prudhoe Bay. Local newspaper columns and letters-to-the-editor demand opening up the Arctic National Wildlife Refuge to slack our energy thirst. A woman from California on a television monitor complains of the expense of filling up her Explorer. "The President needs to do SOMETHING," she implores, her hand squeezing the gas hose so tightly that her knuckles have turned white. Cheap oil is what's needed now, more of it, too. The BP men are ready to help that woman out, ready to drill all the way to the Earth's core if necessary.

Flying to Kodiak Island ("America's second largest island," Hazel had said.) is risky on a good day. This is not a good day. The stewardess had cautioned us before takeoff, "All pukers off the plane now!" The Convair CV-580 from Anchorage bobbed and heaved like a broken roller coaster. I tried to concentrate on my breathing like a Buddhist lama, but all I could think of was that my ex-wife's name was still listed as the primary beneficiary on my life insurance policy. In my clenched fist was a newspaper clipping I had torn out from that day's *Anchorage Times* with the headline, "Rabid Fox Snaps at Barrow Cabbie." "The grader driver warned the cabbie away and straddled (!) the animal with the grader....a rabies quarantine set to expire on Tuesday was extended to April 14. Several rabid foxes have been destroyed this year in Barrow....." I was now in a state that had a rabies quarantine in effect.

When I had the guts to peek out the window, there was only water and sky, waves and clouds. Kodiak's runway ends at the base of a soaring mountain and just when it seemed we would crash into the mountain, the nightmare ride was over. I turned to the fellow in the seat next to me—part-time bluegrass banjo player and a full-time cargo pilot—and bravely said, "That wasn't so bad." He had spent the flight reassuring me with one hair-raising tale of near-death plane rides after another. "When the electricity hit the plane the entire cockpit lit up like fireworks. If I wasn't wearing my seatbelt my head would have smashed through the roof like a ripe pumpkin! I thought I was a goner. Do you listen to Alison Krauss?"

Sometimes the landings are so rough that passengers, who have not collapsed from fright, applaud the cockpit crew, then walk down the stairs onto the icy tarmac delicately carrying their steaming bags of vomit.

I deplane in record time. Inside the tiny airport is another glass case with more dead animals: a 1,400-pound Kodiak bear and a 225-pound Sitka blacktail deer and, as I'll soon see, the walls of my hotel room are dripping with the pelts of blue fox and badgers.

My cabby bailed out of Phoenix ("too many assholes!") for Kodiak eleven years ago, but he barely makes it with the high cost of living in Alaska. "Gas is so high now I can't afford to work full-time." Neil Young strums acoustically in the background on the local NPR station and I spot my first bald eagle before the cabby hits the speed limit. He asks my business and I tell him the standard line: "I'm a writer working on a story." Without hesitation or further questioning he tells me I should get on the radio station and announce my arrival. "The women would like you," he says looking me over like prey. "Of course in Kodiak all we have are 'fours.' No 'tens' up here so you have to lower your standards. But a four plus a six pack is a ten!"

"Thanks," I tell him, "but I'm sure all I would attract would be the wrong women." He's ready for me. "All we have is wrong women in Kodiak!" Ha ha ha ha.

The five-mile ride and the advice cost me nineteen dollars. Russian influence dominates Kodiak. Blue onion domes—the Byzantine architectural flourishes of the Russian Orthodox Church—rise above a huge commercial fishing harbor with several processing plants. Street names include Rezanof, Shelikof, and Ismailov. Downtown is the Alaskan Samovar Inn. The landscape is wild: wide rivers running into a risky sea, ringed by massive mountains. The two main roads out of town dead end at the edge of wilderness. I stop counting eagles at around sixty. Flying and a ferry are the only way off the island. Kodiak's phone book lists fourteen plane companies under the heading of airlines—Sea Hawk, Uyak Air, Homer Air, Highline Air, and so on.

Over breakfast on my first morning in Kodiak, a man from Bristol Bay tells us how to kill a fox or a mink. "You grab him by the tail and snap him like a whip. Breaks its neck every time." He stands up and demonstrates with his napkin. He then tells the story of a buddy who was out on his trap line and tried the same technique on what he didn't know was a wolverine. "That wolverine turned on him and bit him square in the gut. He dropped that tail, pulled out his .357 and Bam! Bam! Emptied the entire chamber." We nod like a team in an agreeable way, in a gesture that says "he had no choice but to kill that damn wolverine," and pass the plate of fried over-easy eggs, sausage, and pancakes around the table.

He continues with the story of how he saved a friend. "I had a dream that he was on his snowmobile and went through the ice. I tried to reach him but he slipped away, right through my fingers. I woke up, jumped in my truck, and rushed over to his house waking him and his wife at three a.m. I told him about my dream and how he had to witness for the Lord. And he did, right then and there." His eyes pool with tears, and there's a terrible silence at the table until a woman guides the topic in a different direction: How snowmobile suits have a tendency to fill up with water, which is why a Kodiak man plunged to his death when he hit a patch of thin ice in his machine. "He never had a chance. He called for help, but there were only teenagers around. They tried to push a skiff out to him, but he couldn't reach it. Really messed up an eighteen-year-old here in town. He was a senior with just a few months until graduation, but after the death he was so broken up he just dropped out of school. I guess from what I hear he's a real mess. Took it real hard like he was responsible."

The men then look over at me to see if I could top their bullet and Bible stories, if I can move the narrative thread in a more dramatic direction. After all, I'm a writer. All I can think of is how an installation of a Zip Drive on my computer killed the monitor and I had to ship it all the way down to San Jose. And how lost and sad that made me feel—vulnerable, too—and how I almost just gave up. I stare down at my soft, pink hands, my limp, carpal-tunnel-ravaged wrists, and decide not to share.

Death, animals, fish runs, weather, boats, and especially planes are common topics in Alaska. Folks are friendly and talkative, as if assessing your potential in an outdoor catastrophe, but above all you have to be able to tell stories, and tell them well. Conversations often begin this way: "I had just killed me a moose and I had a bear nosing around the gut pile in no time. So I killed the bear, too."

Over a delicious meal of fish and chips at Henry's Restaurant I notice the bar is packed even though it's only four in the afternoon. The bar maid could easily trade places with her customers. She is busy tearing up pull tabs and throwing them onto the floor, which is a foot-deep in discarded tabs. A drunk greets me in the universal language of alcohol. " Hey, how are you, buddy? Buy me a little drink?"

I walk back to the hotel in a blizzard and pass a native kid, who looks at me and says, "This wind sucks, man!"

A few days on Kodiak convince me that even though I am technically a middle-aged male, in Alaska I am a boy. After all, I have never killed a large animal, which means I have never skinned a large, warm mammal, or eaten fresh lynx meat, lost several toes to frostbite, or left a buddy to die in a blizzard.

I have never been caught in the jaw with a halibut hook, mauled by a sow bear, or gored by a muskox. I've never fired a gun or tasted fresh whale. I don't even own a pocketknife. Still, I feel invigorated, like I've been harpooned with enough testosterone to last me until deer season (of course I'll be bird-watching during those weeks).

Down below, among the other courageous office workers in their cubicles, I'll return a hero. "I've been up in Alaska," I'll brag. "Up among the wolves, the caribou, and the salmon-choked rivers."

"You do seem different," my co-workers will remark. "But it's only March. Don't the salmon run in June?"

Nevertheless.

On the cab ride back to the Kodiak airport, strong Arctic head winds of 40 knots prevent the cab from going faster than 25 miles per hour. Eagles roost on light poles and church steeples. Incredibly the fishing boats are leaving the harbor for open water. These are tough people. I am not.

This time my cabby is from the Philippines and on his dashboard are two small elephants with their trunks raised. "Elephants are good luck, right?" I ask, trying to keep my mind filled with positive thoughts of diversity.

"Yes, but in Philippines our elephants are wooden not plastic," he says with disgust.

The fare is twenty dollars and despite my generous tip, the cabby doesn't even get out to help unload my luggage. I should have never mentioned the elephants.

"Too cold. Not cold in Philippines!" he yells as he drives off.

I'm left alone in front of the terminal, feeling as far away as I've ever been from the familiar. I listen to the howling wind and notice that the inside walls of my nostrils are beginning to freeze together. As the snow drifts up around my shins. I hear the drone of an airplane in the distance as it banks across the bay to attempt a landing. Inside, my fellow passengers are all standing calmly at the windows to watch. The thought of climbing into that tiny plane brings bile to my throat and an uncomfortable rumbling in my lower intestine. I hustle inside to search for a bathroom.

My Permanent Liminal Space

You never know where life will take you. And that brings me to a Walmart parking lot on an anxiety-producing gray day in central Illinois where snow and Xanax might or might not improve the ambience.

The Illinois location is irrelevant because truthfully I could be in any mid-sized city where generic America is in full frenetic overdrive; where the rough edges of our individual choices have been ground down to our most basic consumptive urges; the commodities of modern living reduced to greasy, sugary mouth feel, impulse bulk buying, soy lattes with sprinkles, all of this dutifully conducted while passively watching flocks of non-migrating geese negotiating four lanes of SUV traffic in a treeless bland tableau of Anywhere USA.

I guess it's probably fortunate that no one breaks it to you early in life that instead of, say, winning a Nobel Prize for Literature, saving white rhinos or curing cancer, you will spend much of your time in uninspiring situations like this; that you will be, as I am this January afternoon, a layabout, idly watching a covey of sparrows foraging amid discarded shopping carts outside my car while I wait for my wife to emerge from the store with necessities for her ninety-seven-year-old mother. I can almost detect grains of sand swishing through my hourglass. Time is running out, but I've been living on borrowed time since I arrived sixty-five years ago on a frigid December evening on the South Side of Chicago.

This bit of avian activity seems so horribly out of place. I mean, there are forests and a river not far from here. Yet, the birds nest in the eaves of Walmart's massive structures and sometimes I even spot them flying inside those buildings, mostly in the gardening section, that part of the store that smells of fertilizer and mulch.

There was a time when I would have reached for a field guide to Illinois birds to conclusively identify these sparrows, of which there seems to be dozens of varieties. I used to travel with such guides, binoculars, and a notebook to record those findings, but it now seems less important to be able to distinguish the subtle markings between a Savannah sparrow and a Vesper sparrow. I'd rather just revel in their movements and their songs, and be blissfully unaware of the obscure colors on their heads.

So I watch these unidentified "lbbs," aka little brown birds, flit and fight over French fries, heels of soggy bread from Subway, and shreds of iceberg lettuce. I'm not opposed to learning new things. I just want to know more about what I already know.

I happen to be parked directly in front of a car that shows the effects of a recent accident. Driver's door is bashed in, the spider web of a cracked passenger window held together with black electrician's tape, and a dented passenger's door held together more or less with a bungy cord. Its windows are tinted so I have no way of knowing if someone is watching *me*.

My doors are secured with electronic locks. I have pepper spray in the arm rest because crime is rampant in these days of COVID, when unemployment and poverty are on the rise. Yet, I would probably forget that I even had the spray if I was suddenly carjacked. There is a security company that patrols the area in a pickup truck, but rent-a-cops have never been reassuring. Anyway, who wants a 15-year-old Subaru without Bluetooth capability?

Some of the people I observe coming and going from Walmart look eerily like the MAGA folks who breached the U.S. Capitol in January. I am not happy about my reflexive prejudice. Still, I see the same sullen, menacing don't-mess-with-me looks I saw on TV that fateful day of insurrection, and the sloppy sweatshirts and beefy Carhartt gear that might or might not conceal a loaded Glock-19.

Stationed at the entrances and exits to the parking lots are the homeless sentries with their cardboard signs that are all coincidentally written in the same typestyle. The homeless, who might be "veterans," might have "cancer," might be "disabled," or might be "starving," sometimes have puppies with them. Because of those cute dogs I have dispensed money and food, but I have become more suspicious when an acquaintance told me he once saw them disembark from a van and disperse over the area, as if they were carpooling to a 9-5 job.

I guess I could look at this moment in the parking lot as wasted time, as an hour that I will wish I had back at the end of my life, but, truthfully, there have been so many of these moments in my six-and-a-half decades that it would be hard to rank one from the other. (Then there are all those lost hours asleep.) I tend to be more cautious than impulsive; more careful than courageous. I am neither a follower or a joiner, and I reside so deeply inside my mind that I crave idleness and quiet space above all else, much to the detriment of perhaps, well, participating in making the world a better place or simply learning a new language.

Yet, it has occurred to me that the definition of wasted time is different at this upper middle age than it might have been earlier in my life, if I was even thinking of it at all back then. Like a veteran quarterback, the game of life has slowed down sufficiently that I can now see the entire playing field. I am craftier, relying more on experience instead of mindless, youthful hormonal-guided risk, to guide me through the myriad of obstacles that confront a human being in his sixties. I guess that translates to not caring quite as much about cooling my heels in a Walmart parking lot. It's not like I was going to split the atom today. Or ever for that matter.

One might assume the opposite: that every second remaining in the next twenty (if I'm lucky) years is itself a precious opportunity to finally accomplish, well, what exactly? I'm forever nagged by the thoroughly American guilt-filled notion of striving to overachieve. I can hear the nagging critics: *How can one watch birds without identifying them or sketching their beaks? How do you observe the homeless yet not interview them for a book about poverty, or pour one's life savings into a shelter for these unfortunates? I mean, how lazy can you get?*

Guilt can be a thoroughly worthless emotion, especially if what you feel guilty about not accomplishing that which you could never possibly accomplish in the first place. At sixty-five, I am what I am, and will always be, and I have the rest of my life to come to terms with what I *have* achieved. But how to evaluate what those achievements are in a country obsessed with accumulation, the Big Splash, the Next New Thing?

My own beloved will return soon, take my hand in hers, and reassure me (once again) that I am fine despite my fears that I am not doing my share to help others. "Well, you help *me* every day," she will say.

Until she returns, I will sit here, in this unlikely location with my eyes wide open. I'm taking it all in—this liminal place of scavenging birds and desperate people—and conclude that what I am seeing is quite glorious, every bit of it, if, that is, I will give it my undivided attention.

How I Failed at Farming…Again

Just before the great Illinois corn-and-soybean harvest begins, it is customary to tell farm-injury stories. These graphic tales of startling disfigurement are told in the poker-faced manner of the heartland Midwesterner, who handles everything life can throw at him—from winning the Illinois State Lottery to a farm foreclosure—in the same way: a nod of the head, a pick of a stubborn callus, possibly a spit of tobacco, and a tight grimace that says, "Oh, well, what can you do?" Grim encounters between man and jagged mechanical parts are usually recounted in machine sheds while the storyteller is engaged in the very activity that led a neighbor to lose a knuckle, a testicle, or half his face.

"Caught his shirt sleeve in the grain auger," the farmer might say, while loading grain into an auger himself. "Ripped off all his clothes and broke about every bone in his body before it spit him out. Lay there quietly for hours before anyone came by. Vultures started circling. Rats, too. The only person within shouting distance was the boss's wife, which is why he kept quiet. He was embarrassed, you know, about being naked in the vicinity of a proper lady."

An auger is a large screw-like mechanism that conveys grain from ground level to the top of one of those tall silver bins that break the flatness of the prairie landscape. Augers are noisy, dangerous, and unforgiving. It's no wonder many a shipment of Midwest grain includes a missing digit. (The only other occupation that loses so many fingers is that of a butcher. Next time you find yourself at the meat counter at your local supermarket, count the fingers on the guy hacking away at ribeyes. You will rarely count to ten.)

Farm-injury stories are useful if for no other reason that they scare the rest of us away from farming. This may explain, in part, why fewer than 3 percent of the workforce farms and the rest of us merrily eat away without exactly knowing where our food originates. (We know milk comes from cows and beef comes from cattle, and that the two animals are somehow related. But what's a steer? And why would one "poll" an Angus?)

If you have a strong stomach and can listen long enough without fainting or retching, you'll find that farm-injury stories have an important underlying message: pay attention. Furthermore, when you think things are going well, pay *extra* attention. By the Midwestern farmer's philosophy, bad is bad, and good will probably turn bad if you don't watch out. Average is ideal.

My brother-in-law summed it up one afternoon while changing one of the massive dual tires on his John Deere combine: "John Jordan had one of these tires fall on top of him. Suffocated him to death. Slowly. He was having a good day…too good."

After twenty-seven years of living out west, I have moved to rural Illinois so my wife can be near her family. When we first arrived, I begin bragging about my previous farm experience at a dairy in Michigan's Upper Peninsula, where I was employed as an "assistant dairy herdsman." Impressive as the title sounds, all it meant was that I toiled like an indentured servant seven days a week, twelve hours a day, without regular coffee breaks. During daylight hours, I milked sixty messy cows—twice—and helped with the unrelenting field work. Nighttime was reserved for locating strays in nearby forests, where they loved to play hide-and-seek, and chasing them back to their pasture. Any remaining time was usually spent on my back studying the insides of my eyelids. For compensation, I was given a drafty farm house, the princely sum of six hundred dollars a month, and unlimited supply of high-fat milk and red meat.

This was twenty years ago, during my failed back-to-the-land period. My experience was hardly the pastoral ideal I'd had in mind. I'd pictured more of a Wendell Berry essay: farming with draft horses; growing weed- and insect-free patches of organic carrots, peaches, and tomatoes; working in harmony with like-minded people who never had trouble reaching consensus. There would be black Labrador retrievers named Molly, with red kerchiefs around their necks, frolicking in poppy-covered meadows. Someone else would cook large, stew-like meals and bake round loaves of brown bread. I would have ample time to write poetry and to learn to play the dulcimer. In the afternoon, I would take two-hour naps in handmade Guatemalan hammocks. (That's as far as I got in my pre-dairy fantasy. Actually, imagining the naps, stews, and homemade bread was usually good enough.)

Reality, of course, was something else altogether. Squatting beside a manure-covered cow and squeezing her teats as she tries to kick in your head is as glamorous as it sounds. Getting slapped in the face with the same cow's urine-soaked tail is also high on my list of experiences never to repeat. Dairy cows are extremely stubborn, and also bony in the hips, so hitting them is a bad idea, and the reason why so many dairy farmers break their hands. But the most valuable lesson I learned was: never stand directly behind a cow when she coughs. Their bowels are looser than creamed corn.

Heavy-machinery breakdowns are common on farms, and my mechanical skills were nonexistent as those of most city kids. Whenever one of the tractors I was driving malfunctioned, all I could do was stand around and fetch wrenches for my boss. My status further deteriorated when I valiantly refused to spray the herbicide on the corn (I was reading Rachel Carson's *Silent*

Spring at the time) or participate in coyote hunts, which were popular among the farm hands. Nor did it help when I remarked that I thought the artificial insemination guy seemed to be enjoying his work with the herd a little too much. (He was a friend of my boss.)

After nine months of mutual torture and near decapitations, I had developed a serious case of silage cough, everything I owned stank of Holsteins, and all those meals of rich dairy products had caused my cholesterol level to soar. At this time, my employer and I reached an agreement. I would leave in two weeks (sooner if I wanted). In return, I could look for another job, preferably a nonagricultural one, in another state. And he would let me. I thought this was a great arrangement.

I didn't tell my Illinois brother-in-law that I was a dismal failure in my former agrarian life, but I suspect he could see how green I was. Farmers can gauge your mechanical competence the way animals can sense fear. They see it in the way you wield a throttle, pop a clutch, or pull a choke. They can take one look at your hands and tell if you've ever dissembled a carburetor or torn apart an axle. My hands were soft and pink, like those you might see on a Jergen's lotion commercial. My only calluses were from playing my guitar and pushing a computer mouse.

My brother-in-law put me to work mowing acres of lawn and walking the endless fields cutting down weeds with curve-bladed scythes that could just as easily hack apart an ankle or shin. Shatter cane was sprouting up among the seed corn, and invasive water hemp had jumped into a soybean field from a nearby drainage ditch. This was hot, humid, itchy work without bottled mineral water. For a week afterward, my delicate hands and arms were covered with welts and rashes. It was hard to use my computer mouse. But I didn't dare complain because, as any farmer will tell you, "things could be worse." After all, I still had my thumbs and both my testicles.

Sure, I had made a few minor errors, especially while mowing. Who else could get a riding lawn mower stuck on a flat piece of Illinois ground? Who else would run the mower blade over a tree stump at the exact moment his brother-in-law was cautioning him about having the blade too low? I missed slicing through electrical lines and toppling rosebushes by the thinnest of margins.

Still, because I was family, I was given a second chance. Come harvest time, I got a promotion. My new job would be to haul soybeans from the field. My brother-in-law would fill two grain bins from the combine. All I had to do was hook a tractor up to the wagons, drive them half a mile to the farm, rev up the dreaded auger, dump my loads, and watch the pale brown beans rise up into the silver bins. Most Illinois farm kids could perform the same task effortlessly by the sixth grade. But before my brother-in-law turned me loose upon the golden prairie, he felt compelled to tell me a story.

"A guy climbed up into a bin to smooth out the pile. A beautiful day, just like today. He was just about done, and the harvest was going great. Bean prices were going up, too. That should have warned him. Anyhow, he got too close to the center of the bean pile and was caught in a whirlpool. Beans just swallowed him up. Drowned in his own bounty. He was still holding on to his shovel when they found him. He was about your age. Kinda looked like you, too…Well, we'd better get to work."

I failed on my first attempt to line up the wagons next to the auger. The next three tries were no better, but finally I was able to negotiate all the various throttles and brakes and on-off switches and maneuver the wagons into position. *Not bad for my first time out*, I thought. But I didn't dare celebrate or even vaguely smile. I dumped my two loads and headed back to the field for more.

"How did things go?" my brother-in-law asked over the walkie-talkie.

"Oh, so-so. About middling," I answered.

"Good," he replied.

I loved talking on that walkie-talkie.

When I reached the field, I unhooked the two empty wagons and attached the two full ones that were waiting for me. Then I noticed a radio in the cab of the tractor I was driving. In hindsight, I should have ignored the shiny dials. But it was around two o'clock in the afternoon and *Fresh Air* was just coming on NPR. So I flipped the switch, turned the volume up high, and settled in for the short ride back to the farm. A bubbling Terry Gross was interviewing political consultant David Gergen about his new memoir, and there I was, bringing in the crops in America's Heartland, just like a figure from a Grant Wood painting.

I turned into the farm driveway like a conquering hero, and, to my delight, lined up the wagons on the very first try. This was getting easy. My Michigan misfortunes must have been just bad luck or poor supervision. I adjusted my very cool Amish straw hat and pulled on my dirty work gloves, feeling very authentic. I was in control of large machinery manufactured by union laborers. I was *farming*. Now, couldn't I allow myself to feel just a little bit satisfied? Must all traces of ego be tempered in the Midwest?

I unloaded the first wagon, careful to keep my sleeves rolled up and stand clear of the deadly auger, which was spinning like mad and calling my name. Attached to the lower end of the auger was a basket-like contraption that caught the beans as they fell from the wagon. In my haste to get back to Terry Gross, I had neglected to raise the basket out of the way before moving the second wagon into place. As the tractor rolled forward, I heard the unmistakable sound of crumpling aluminum, not unlike the crushing of an enormous beer can. Looking hesitantly back at what I had done, I felt as if I had lost a testicle.

As if on cue, my brother-in-law's voice crackled on the walkie-talkie:. "How's it going?"

"Not good," I answered.

"Great," he replied.

"No, you don't understand," I said.

"Copy that again?"

My brother-in-law delivered his lecture in the machine shed. His words punctuated by the angry sounds of a sledge hammer pounding metal. "Didn't I tell you: just when you think things are going well is when you should be pay the closest attention?" All I could do was hang my head in shame and hand in my walkie-talkie.

The next day, I returned to supervised mowing.

Elvis Imitators on Spring Break

If you are fortunate to arrive at the gates of midlife, you will have no doubt encountered an Elvis imitator along the way. At any given moment, in this diverse country of ours, a man is wearing a sequined suit and singing "Love me tender, love me true." My theory of an endless supply of Elvis crooners extends to the endless loop of music that we hear in malls, elevators, and restaurants. With unrelenting regularity, the assault on our aural senses includes "Yesterday," "Take it Easy," Crocodiles Rock," and "You're So Vain." These songs shaped and transformed our wasted youth as we mostly headed to the country, where we read Hesse, wrote earnest passages in our journals, and phoned home for money.

But now, thirty years and ten thousand listens later, as I wander through a mega store in search of Tums and Tylenol, the lure of "I want to sleep with you in the desert tonight," is not as appealing as a good night's sleep on a firm Serta.

Which, believe it or not, brings us to Ft. Myers Beach, Florida, at the height of that American rite of debauchery known as Spring Break. And man do those college kids need a break. They've been in school for an entire month and half.

It was at such a week of throngs, thongs, and bongs that I attended my first Elvis imitator concert. The venue was a more subdued time-share resort of quiet middle-aged couples and retirees that featured two pools, a hot tub, shuffleboard court, several outdoor grills, and thousands of confused lizards darting in and out of palm and banana trees. Lincolns, Chryslers, and Fords owned by heat-seeking Midwesterners escaping the wind chill from Illinois, Ohio, Minnesota, and Wisconsin packed the parking lot. Shirtless, barrel-chested men in sandals prowled the grounds, their bronze bellies stuffed with beef and bourbon. With cigar stubs propped in their mugs and bottomless drinks in hand, the men were proof that you can become successful in insurance and plastics. Maybe agricultural chemicals, too.

"So Elvis lives," says an elderly man, without a trace of irony. We are standing together on a balcony overlooking the gathering crowd of a baker's dozen waiting for the King to make his appearance. Some are quite drunk. We watch Elvis's assistant, who I later find out is a disgruntled employee at the resort, tinker with the portable sound system with all the joy of cleaning a litter box. He mutters something that might rhyme with "duck" and then Elvis himself comes out of a nearby restroom, making final adjustments to his wide collar, sheer scarf, metal-framed glasses, and white leather shoes (a familiar accessory in south Florida). In addition, he wears a classic sequined jumpsuit—also white—with bell-bottomed pants, and his underwear (pallid briefs) is showing. On the back of his jumpsuit is a painting of a Phoenix that is apparently rising. Elvis is around forty years old with long, jet-black hair, which I believe to be his own, and the trademark mutton chop sideburns.

"Hi, I'm Wayne Newton," he quips. "I'm going to sing some Elvis standards and some not-too-well-known songs."

He gives a cue and looks over at his sound man, who mutters and sorts through some CDs. Elvis says something under his breath, walks over, and pushes a button. Out of the small speaker comes his introduction: the theme song from "2001: A Space Odyssey." He picks up his microphone and sings "Good Time Charlie's Got the Blues," not exactly an Elvis standard. He quickly follows up with "Hound Dog" and "My Way." Elvis has a good voice and sings with passion, but when he comes to the line, "Let the record show, I took the blows," he steps on a plastic ashtray that shatters, the largest part scuttling out onto the beach. "Shit, sorry about that," he says.

It occurs to me that this imitation is not of the svelte, throbbing Elvis who performed in the "Ed Sullivan Show" in 1956, and was only allowed to be shown from the waist up to avoid uncontrollable sexual urges by teenage fans. What I am watching from the balcony of the time share is Elvis toward the end: the bloated, gut-over-belly star, heavy in girth and step, rumored to be hooked on a pharmacy's worth of pills. Elvis on the edge, just before August 16, 1977, when, at the Graceland mansion at the age of forty-two, he finally keeled over while sitting on the toilet, a victim of cardiac arrhythmia. "The king is dead," said John Lennon. "But rock 'n roll will never die. Long live the king."

A woman with blue hair and one of the largest diamonds I've ever seen walks up to me and hisses, "Having an Elvis imitator cheapens the place."

I think back to earlier in the week at the Lani Kai, the well-used beachside motel where the Spring Breakers crash. A sign advertised, "Braids, Beads, and Cornrows by Tara." A burly bouncer and his posse turned cars away from the parking lots with a stern, "Stay out! We're Full!" This was on busy Estero Boulevard, the traffic-pedestrian clogged main artery for the island, in fact, the only road on and off Ft. Myers Beach. Knots of drunk and rowdy college kids roamed the T-shirt stalls, beachwear shops, bars, and restaurants. Self-esteem was high. A new Cadillac Escalade with counter-intuitive twirling gold rims, tucked ebony leather seats, and a dashboard DVD player queued up at the McDonald's drive through, the latest forgettable hip hop anthem blaring out with a bass so deep that the car windows quivered. Near the Mango Fruit

Stand, which featured red snapper, Gulf shrimp, and sample wedges of ruby red grapefruit, a Chevy Blazer prowled by with ten young, bare-chested men, who leaned out the windows, licking their lips like lizards, and yelling at a group of coeds, "Oh yes, girls, that's all you!" A woman of around 19 teetered by on high-heeled clogs and outfitted in a skimpy bikini that had to contain less than a handful of Lycra. She clung to a drunk boy of around the same age, who was saying earnestly, "You mean, like where I was born, or like where I'm living now?"

••••

The Elvis imitator's signature move is to jerk both hands back as if pulling the reins on a team of oxen. Then he staggers for effect. He did this reining-in routine on several numbers, including "Glory, Glory, Hallelujah," a piece that seemed to spellbound the audience. Not once did he dance or swivel his hips, even on "I'm All Shook Up," and certainly not on "Let It Be" or "Help Me through the Night." And when he sang "The Wonder of You," the line "you give me hope and consolation" came out "Hope and constipation." Nobody noticed.

••••

That afternoon back behind Lani Kai, on a beach littered with beer cans and broken lounge chairs, a local disc jockey introduced an act called the "Fellatio Brothers," that he said were New York City police men and, thus, somehow linked in a positive, patriotic thread to events of September 11.

"Who knows what 'fellatio' means," asked the disc jockey. A Bronx cheer when up. A few people waved American flags. The Fellatio Brothers, dressed in disco gear and wearing Afro wigs, then strutted forth to Stevie Wonder's opening funk hook in "Superstition." They proceeded to strip down to g-strings for the large crowd, which became so thick that I couldn't see everything that was happening. But I do remember seeing the woman with the blue hair and the big rock. She was reaching for one of the Fellatio Brothers with both hands extended.

Nearby, identically dressed couples with metal detectors and trowels probed the sand for pocket changes and jewelry. Children with plastic pails and shovels built forts and sand models of starfish. Young guys with yellow and aqua boa constrictors wrapped around their necks promenaded up and down the coast. A kid sat by himself punishing a guitar with a pick and singing at the top range of his voice. Pleasure boats bobbed off-shore, pari-sails drifted overhead, and young men with washboard abs maneuvered jet skis at breakneck speeds, sometimes flipping them over in the waves.

Flocks of laughing gulls and black skimmers rested like decoys in whatever sandy real estate was left to them. They all faced west toward the receding tide. I thought of the lyrics to a Jesse Winchester song, "Biloxi," a tune you will never hear in Costco or Walmart. "Down around Biloxi, pretty girls are swimming in the sea. Oh, they look like sisters of the ocean." The world seemed soft and perfect in a dreamy way. The temperature was 85 degrees with little humidity and no bugs.

In Florida, depending on your age, you can feel young again—even reborn—or, suddenly too old. Even on the beach during Spring Break there are ominous reminders of mortality: men totting oxygen tanks through the sand, and women in post-stroke awkwardness. Ambulance sirens are always wailing, signaling another heart attack or broken hip. Forty-six is not so old anymore. In fact, it is downright vigorous.

But then, just down the beach toward the Lani Kai, forty-six can seem over the hill. All one has to do is stroll past the endless volleyball games with the bouncing girls, who are now younger than your children, but nonetheless alluring in their inadequate bikinis, their navels framed with sunburst henna tattoos and punctured with silver posts and rings. They have pre-childbirth hips and 18-inch waists, and perfect breasts without a sign of sag. (It doesn't help that the bikinis are often flesh colored and the girls look naked from a distance.) Of course they don't give you a glance, even if you are like me and jog forty minutes a day with five-pound weights with a respectable 34-inch belt-line, and you can finally afford a trip to Florida.

But I will say middle age has its advantages. People either take you more seriously or they ignore you altogether (see above). It's like you are given a temporary pass, a breather between the angst-filled biologically-driven days of your first forty-odd years, and the more careful and thoughtful and just plain tired years of your last three decades…maybe four. You no longer hitchhike. No one challenges you to a fistfight. Television commercials are more likely to fascinate instead of repel. Coffee doesn't taste as good so you drink less of it. Vanity falls off away, which can have its drawbacks (watch the eye brow hairs, men). You can't stay up all night and discuss Kafka, which is such a relief. And you realize that those girls in the bikinis are probably more trouble for you than they are worth. Like what in God's name would we talk about? Still, it did make my ego soar when a gas station clerk in Alabama said I reminded her of Mick Jaggar. "There's something about you," she said, smiling with that adorable Dixie drawl. I can only hope she meant a *young* Mick Jaggar.

••••

In the middle of "Suspicious Minds" it becomes apparent that the wide belt Elvis wears is much too big. He tugs and pulls and finally takes it off to the bawdy cheers of an elderly woman in an unflattering halter. Tourists march up to Elvis and flash their disposable cameras and point their camcorders. During a rather rousing performance of "Jailhouse Rock," in which Elvis dramatically gives his scarf to a young girl, several people rise up from their beach chairs to dance. One woman swings her granddaughter by her arms in a wide arc. The music ends and Elvis stands there looking not so much like the pop star, but more like a perspiring overweight lounge singer. "Thank you, thank you very much. We're going to take a short break. My assistant will come around with a bucket. Please give generously."

I leave just before the second set. I am not alone. A medley of "CC Rider" and "Nothing But A Hound Dog" follow me to my room. I lie in bed caressed by Gulf winds and, with the sound muted, passively watch the Real Estate Network. Across the screen flash scene after scene of lavish interiors, sprawling golf courses, spacious bays, non-native landscaping, waterfalls, and exuberant middle-aged couples riding bicycles. The Olde Naples Seaport had "openings from $1.75 mil." Building 2 was "just released" at the Twin Dolphins from the $700's. "Last chance for waterfront elegance" at The Dunes, "from the $300's to over $2 million." There was still time to buy time at Rookery Pointe, Herons Glen, Pelican Landing, Pelican Isle, and Bayshore Estates (just $799,000). If Bayshore was too expensive, Paradise Village offered a "Key-Wester Model" for $789,000.

The lonely sound of six people applauding snaps me out of my stupor long enough to reach for the remote and turn off the television. After his finale of "Heartbreak Hotel," Elvis asks the audience, "Did you like my show?" I look out the window to where the crowd is begging for an encore, but Elvis and his reluctant helper can't seem to get the sound system working again. Finally, everyone drifts back to their rooms.

Elvis was a hit. My last morning at the resort I noticed a flyer posted in the main office announcing Elvis's return the following Thursday night. But by the time he reappeared, I already driven the 1,400 miles north to Illinois, where the trees were still bare and the icy wind took my breath away.

My Extra Year

All of last year I thought I was a year older than I actually was. For twelve frantic months, with my fiftieth birthday looming larger by the hour, I walked around with a bad attitude. "I am forty-eight. You got a problem with that!?" No one did. Neither waitresses, Kinko's clerks, nor my long-suffering tabby cat would pick a fight. In fact, no one noticed the new chip on my shoulder. I realized being middle aged is mostly a time when one is largely ignored.

Still, it was a heady time. The entire year I tried more than ever to pay closer attention. I wanted to taste and feel the texture of the world around me; to be one of the smart and informed who begins each conversation with "Guess what I heard on NPR?" and, "I just read a fascinating article in the science section of the *Times*..."

With mortality looking back at me in the mirror, I had so much to learn in so little time. For example, what to make of the rise of male enhancement products? With only two quick years remaining until the big 50, I desperately sought the answers to all the world's great questions. I debated internally whether PBS was too liberal and FOX News was too conservative. I sat as close as I could to my 12-inch television set to dutifully read CNN's ticker tape of tragedy crawling along the bottom of my screen. I learned that Utah still had active polygamists, North Dakota had "killer" blizzards, and California had either too much or too little rain. I learned we were all suspects. Satellite trucks could appear outside our houses at any minute.

In airport waiting rooms, gas stations, and even in doctors' offices, I was trapped in an unrelenting loop of sound bites and images. Commentators commented, lawyers lobbied, and analysts analyzed. Nobody could agree on anything. I was exhausted trying to keep up with them. I developed "bomb fatigue." Bombs went off on crowded buses in Israel and then tanks rolled into Gaza, and then bombs went off on crowded buses in Israel and tanks... Scott Peterson enters the courtroom. Michael Jackson waves to his fans. Muslims gather and scream outside mosques. Lawyers and their clients disembark from black SUV's. Denials came just before admissions. Then came tearful apologies on the steps of courthouses. In the background, Kenny Chesney crooned, the Dow stumbled then rallied then stumbled, Hannity scolded, and through it all there continued to be persistent drizzle in Seattle and severe thunderstorms in Kansas.

When my birthday rolled around this time I was ecstatic to find that I was forty-eight, again. (Of course, that meant I would be forty-nine, again, too. At this rate I might even make it to AARP, Social Security, and Medicare.) The age of fifty would be delayed. *Wow, a entire extra year*, I thought. However, this time around I didn't want to act so desperate and I certainly did want to cut down on tracking current events.

I had a lot of thinking to do. But first I needed to celebrate. I bought a new mattress and immediately slept better. So did my two cats. I switched from Starbuck's House Blend coffee to Folgers Columbian. (Now that I had more time there was no reason to go gourmet. And I needed to cut corners if I was going to live longer.) But what to do with this unexpected gift? I began a diary titled "Journal of an Aging Baby Boomer."

"Today I am forty-eight years old. To mark the day I am beginning a journal of sorts, a way of documenting a middle-aged man living in the American Heartland on his run up to the touchstone age of fifty. I hope to write down thoughts and observations on my health, my mind, and what it means to be an American in the beginning of this century."

Then I questioned my chosen profession of writing.

"Why am I not more excited about writing? Why am I not creating more work? Why not more ideas? I am also steering away from controversial subjects. When I was younger I plunged right in without thinking. Is this a sign of age, or of cowardice, or simply weariness? Does creativity come less often as one ages or am I running dry?"

But the journal seemed too narcissistic. Nothing new in *Boomer expresses his angst*. Ugh, what a cliché. I needed to turn off the babbling media, get outside my mind (and off the new bed), and plunge my tender hands into the gritty texture of the real world.

At luck would have it, I was at work on a profile of an independent radio station owner, a dying breed of entrepreneur. His station was located in a squat, run-down, and poorly ventilated building on the edge of a farming town that resembled a bad haircut. We'll call the owner "Ed." He slept on a couch at the station and the place was a mess, but he and his station were well respected in the region. Ed was idealistically committed to playing unknown Americana, blues, and folk artists. Because of a weak transmitter, listeners would strategically park their vehicles in the nearby fields to bring in the station's signal. Although he had been interviewed many times, I explained to him that I practiced *immersion journalism* and I would be around much more than a beat reporter. And I wanted to know everything about his life, past, present, and future. (I am always amazed that people agree to these kinds of requests from strangers.)

On my initial visit, just as we were getting started, one of the station's major sponsors came in, a man who owned a barbeque joint. He suggested we all have a drink at a downtown tavern, one of those ubiquitous main street bars often named The Alibi or The Office. It was 10 a.m., and the bar was far from empty, a fact that always surprises me. Older men wearing feed caps sat on stools nursing beers and Bloody Marys. The music was deafening. Ed and the barbeque guy ordered Milwaukee's Best, which, with a little research, I later found *not* to be Milwaukee's best. I nursed a ginger ale on the rocks.

This was the perfect start to my extra year. *Here I am*, I marveled, *among the salt of the earth*, sitting in a cavernous bar before noon on a weekday in the middle of Illinois with a group of men of whom I had nothing in common. The atmosphere dripped with authenticity and a mushroom cloud of secondhand cigarette smoke. The lyrics of Credence, Bob Seger, and Garth—their rock and roll anthems to the working stiff—blared from the sound system. The BBQ man and Ed were deep into their second or third round of beers. Ed was chain-smoking GNC's. Someone bought me another ginger ale. I took notes.

I soon struck up a conversation with a factory worker who told me that his son called him in a panic a couple of nights before. "He'd agreed to watch a Burmese python while the guy that owned it went overseas. My son's a snake lover by nature, always loved to catch garters and racers along the farm ditches. He once owned a boa, but it got too big for the apartment he was living in at the time, the landlord had little kids you know, so he had to have it put down. The local vet never killed a snake before; he was strictly a cat and dog doc, maybe a bird or gerbil now and then, so he charged him a hundred bucks. Took a lot of drugs to finally do it in. Was kind of a messy deal I heard. Anyway, my son notices that the python, which is huge—long as this bar here— is kind of quiet. Stops eating. My son would throw the mice in the cage and nothing would happen. The mice would just look up at my son like they were asking, 'Well, when am I going to die?' Of course, mice always look like that, kind of permanently nervous like rabbits. This goes on for about a week, until two nights ago. My son comes home after his swing shift at Kraft and Holy Shit! There's a whole mess of tiny snakes coming out of that python. It's like someone turned on a faucet but instead of water out comes a mess of snakes. Like twitching pencils moving in all directions. His living room rug is covered with em! He calls me, out of his mind by now, and I rush over with some burlap sacks and we scoop 'em up the best we can—don't know if we got all of 'em— and take 'em down to the lake. Hope they can swim. Anyway, my son, poor guy, he's pretty shaken up. Plans on living with me for awhile. No more snakes for him. I guess I'll deal with that python tomorrow, or the day after. I tell you, it was a hell of deal. " He drained the last of his beer, said goodbye, and left.

By now it was approaching noon. When I looked over at Ed, his buddy, and the increasing stack of bottles, I could tell my interview wasn't going to happen on this day. I handed him my card, said goodbye, and headed out the door.

The sunlight was a shock, like leaving a movie matinee and forgetting the time of day. I felt centered again, wrapped up in the afterglow of a good story, the under-the-radar narrative of which I am quite sure would never appear in what passes for mainstream popular culture. I craved more.

So for the next few months I avoided most forms of media and, instead, began to listen to other people's voices. What were their passions? In a prison yard, I participated in a charity Crop Walk with more than one hundred female inmates. There were nineteen-year-old murderers and other women, who simply summed up their incarcerations by saying, "I've done some bad things." In their own words, they recounted how drugs, alcohol, and usually the wrong boyfriends led them to doing hard time. "This is a surreal dream, being in prison. This shows what can happen when you lose your focus." They held hands and smoked as they circled the yard raising money for various charities. Afterwards we gathered in a makeshift auditorium to eat shoestring potato chips from Dixie cups. One inmate sang, "I want Jesus to be my friend. I want Jesus to walk with me." Another made an impromptu speech. "There is so much evil in the world. We need to leave all that hate and anger behind us." As I was checked through countless locked gates back into freedom, the assistant warden said, "They're like our children, and they test us daily. But today they did great."

The next month I was on the Mississippi River with a band of idealistic twenty-year olds, whose simple goal was to clean up all the decades of trash accumulated on the shores and islands of that over-worked river. We sped back and forth in small powerboats, reclaiming 55-gallon barrels (one labeled "Prep-N-Kote"), shopping carts, tires, and refrigerators. The work was strenuous, but rewarding. To my surprise the river water was as warm as a freshly poured bath. I thought of that famous saying about the river: "too thick to drink and too thin to plow."

Afterwards we gathered in a beat-up houseboat in a hidden cove for sandwiches and drinks. The stereo was cranked up with the latest tunes from Britney and Rage Against the Machine. I was exhausted, covered in Mississippi silt and mud. But I could easily picture spending the whole summer with the crew. They were having the time of their lives. I asked Chad, the founder of the six-year-old cleanup group, what the Mississippi River meant to him. His eyes lit up as he watched the river.

"It means everything. It's my life. Now I'm in awe of it. How the bluffs change, the islands and different sloughs. It's a sense of freedom to me."

I felt as if I had finally tapped into the real frequency of the nation. And the more I embraced the world around me the more that world revealed its treasures. Stories were everywhere, in nursing homes, in pick-up trucks, on forest trails, and in museums. I held the velvety hand of a 104-year-old woman, and the wet bodies of ring-neck snakes and mole salamanders. I gave guitar lessons to ten-year olds, guiding their fingers across the fret board. I sang "I Want To Be A Cowboy's Sweetheart" and "What A Wonderful World" every week to an Alzheimer's group. Inspired by Chad, I regularly picked up trash along the roads in my own town. In the afternoons, neighborhood children came knocking on my front door, holding buckets containing toads. "Stephen, look what we found! Look at the toadies!" And I did.

To my dismay, the extra year would pass quicker than all the ones that came before. Or so it seemed. Eventually the long, humid nights, filled with the buzzing of cicadas and the calling of frogs, were soon replaced with falls rains, bare tree limbs, and endless skeins of geese. On Thanksgiving afternoon of my second forty-eighth year, I am in the company of a man I'll call Orlen. He takes me on his secret path to the river, down among the wiliest coons and possums, the towering hickories and oaks, right down to where the century-old snappers lie in warm mud and the nasty water snakes coil on overhangs like giant springs. Orlen, a semi-retired bricklayer, is almost eighty, but on most days he can outwork anyone from my Boomer generation. The week before I had seen him in town setting bricks for a new entryway. With eyes twinkling, he yelled out, "Come over here, son, and see what regular people do for a living."

Not long after I moved here and met him, Orlen quickly dismissed me as "too smart," The implication is hardly flattering: I'm soft, a damned writer no less, and much too thoughtful to be of much use in a blue-collar Illinois town. I was not offended. All my life I've moved back and forth between the worlds of white- and blue-collar labor, and the good and bad people that inhabit both. After almost a half century, spent in nine states, I feel as comfortable in a small town café as I do at a university poetry reading. Hard work has never bothered me either, although I do hope my ditch-digging days are behind me.

Today on this freezing, low-light day, while much of the nation is asleep in its Lazy-Boys, stuffed on pie and tripped out on tryptophan, Orlen patrols his 300 acres of wild river frontage like a blue tick, his nose to the ground and his eyes looking in all directions. He had spotted me on the county road, doing my thirty-minute-after-meal-power-walk in spotless white Nikes and my four-hundred dollar leather jacket, trying to keep my weight from busting two hundred. Soon I find myself winded, in a failing attempt to keep up with the old man, who is built like a pro football linebacker and walks as fast as a gazelle. I can feel odd, high-pitched impulses in my chest, what I'm convinced is the beginnings of an eventual heart attack, but pride will not let me complain to Orlen, who wouldn't care anyway. *Regular people don't whine.* Orlen wears three flannel shirts over a V-neck T-shirt, jeans, and Wellington boots. No hat. No gloves. *Regular people don't freeze.* He chews on an unlit cigar and he's not afraid to spit.

Old growth poison ivy vines trip me up. The jagged branches of fallen oaks and sycamores bark my ankles. The sky is pink and giant snow clouds are push down from Canada. All the good weather is about used up. I can feel the temperature drop with each minute, but Orlen is anxious to show me something, he promises, that will change my life.

"My son's down there," he points, toward a impenetrable thicket of briar. "It's bow season. We best leave him alone." Shots echo from across the other bank. Before I can ask, Orlen says, "That's the Baker kid. I let him hunt my land if he cleans up his beer cans." Orlen grew up hunting anything that moved down in southern Indiana, around French Lick. Fox hunting was his specialty. "I got to where I could smell them. Red, grey. Didn't matter."

I had heard about the traps along the river, where Orlen baits turtles with chicken livers. He might even have the 200-pound alligator snapping turtle he's rumored to keep in a cage in the shallows. He says the turtle climbed out of the Mississippi River and walked east through more than a hundred miles of corn and soy to settle here in central Illinois.

"Hey, Orlen," I ask. "Whatever happened to that big snapper you had?"

"He's in the freezer. When I cleaned him, I found this eight-pound channel catfish inside…and an unopened six-pack of Pepsi. But good meat."

After a half hour my new Nikes are coal-colored. The river's water level is the same height as the shore, just a place where the mud gets deeper. A leopard frog jumps over my shoulder, its round tympanum gleaming like a third eye. I still hear geese overhead, but the branches of the forest have formed a dark cathedral and I can't see the sky anymore. Dusk has altered all my senses. The occasional rifle shots sound like something I would hear in a dream. I'm no longer sure I am here at all. We enter the deepest part of the bottomland. Orlen keeps chattering away—something about spotting little honey bears in the woods and maybe a cougar or two—but his words are soon replaced by the sound of running water and the first barred owl of the night. "Who cooks for you?" it wonders over and over without an answer.

I almost crash into Orlen, who stands at the water's edge. Fresh snow flakes coat his shoulders. "Here, right here. Can you feel it?" he asks impatiently, looking down at our muddy feet. "It's right under us."

"*What's* under us?," I ask, looking around.

"The pipeline." Orlen says proudly, as if taking credit for it. "There's oil shooting up from the Gulf of Mexico right below where we're standing. Runs north all the way to Chicago. It's moving under here—thousand of barrels every hour. The oil off-loads at Texas City, runs through Louisiana, Arkansas, Missouri, and into Illinois, up that hill we come down, right across my back yard. You had no idea did you?" Then he walks away to check his traps.

Orlen's last question is more of a challenge than a query. He wants me to understand that he possesses important knowledge, too. And that a guy with no college education, who has never read the *Times*, now owns hundreds of acres and a gorgeous brick house, and has a valuable resource coursing through his property like an artery from the earth. All of this was accomplished, he was saying, with muscles and twelve-hour days. Over and over again, year after year, the way regular people do it.

I brush away the fresh snow off a stump and sit down. In the distance I see the glow of Orlen's cigar as he pulls his cages up from the river. I have no desire to see what is inside. The Canadian front was upon us and snow fell silently into the river. In a few days I would turn forty-nine, certainly for the last time. I tried to think of what might be in store for me in ten, or even five, years. I had no idea. Physically, at this age, whatever was going to lead to my death—cancer, stroke, heart attack—was already well defined. An abnormal cluster of cells. Blocked aorta. Aneurysm. The list is endless. So is that more unpredictable one. But it was too late to turn back now. I felt I was just getting to the good parts.

"Are you coming or you going to just sit there *thinking*?" Orlen was staring at me, a twitching burlap bag slung over his shoulder

"I'm coming," I answered. "Slowly, but I'm coming along."

It was when I stood up, that I finally felt it. Orlen was right all along. The earth *was* throbbing, just beneath my feet, true and steady, like all of our hearts beating together in unison.

Young Chicago Boy Talks to God

On State Street, just past the Wig Center—its window filled with plastic heads of Afros and page boys—I begin to talk to God. Not out loud like so many people do in this city. Or the way the devoted do when they bow their heads in churches and synagogues. My God is an interior voice, a running dialogue only the two of us can hear. Today I am walking with my mother to Marshall Field's. She doesn't know God shares the sidewalk stride for stride with us. The three of us approach Wabash Avenue. The trains rumble overhead on the elevated tracks and God talks right back to me. He says to tell him a story. So I tell him one of the secrets I've never told my mom: the time an impeccably dressed businessman, using his briefcase as a shield, walked his hand up my thigh on the rush-hour Red Line el. The businessman had me trapped against the window, his leg resting warm against mine. He stared ahead the whole time pretending to be a normal commuter. I finally jumped up, pushing past the standing-room-only crowd, and exiting at an unfamiliar stop. Why did I begin to shake? Why tears? God says it wasn't my fault. These things can happen to a boy. That's when I tell him sometimes it takes all my willpower not to burst into a thousand pieces of glass. He says that is certainly a possibility, but advises against it.

God knows I am a Peeping Tom, staring through the security bars of our first-floor apartment across the alley into a basement window, where a woman undresses each night at about eleven. Bras and panties and whatever hides beneath them are my passion. I don't know why yet but something is stirring inside me…and under the covers. God knows this but says nothing. I tell Him I think I am in love with the woman. He says go to sleep, He's tired.

Marshall Field's is the store where my mother tries on dresses, suits, and sweater sets for hours while I escape down the escalator toward the new color televisions. When the clerks asks if I am alone or if I might be lost, I reply that my mother is on Third Floor, Women's Wear. Inside I am saying, "You gotta problem with that? Bug off!" I am that way: tougher on the inside. Other kids, black and white, and all the hues in between, also make their way to the appliances floor to watch Bugs Bunny and Wiley Coyote run, screech, and explode from a hundred screens. We never talk to each other, but we are all part of the Wait-For-Mother Tribe, whose initiation involves long bus and subway rides so our mothers can check out the latest fashions. We are promised Wimpies burgers and Jay's potato chips, fresh roasted peanuts at Montgomery Ward's, and maybe, if we are especially well behaved, we might go to an old theater that shows news reels during the day. It is winter. Our uniforms are frayed corduroy jackets and cotton stocking caps, hopelessly inadequate against Lake Michigan's arctic air that sucks the warmth from our bodies. We are wind-chill kids, all of us, with the patience of the stoic stone lions that guard the Art Institute.

To onlookers it may look I am glued to the cartoons, a ten-year-old wasting time and erasing brain cells, but I am actually talking to God. He likes television, too. He helps me sort out what it means to be a thin-shouldered boy in the city of broad shoulders: A city divided into neighborhoods, which are further divided by race and ethnicity. We Chicagoans know the unmarked borders; know how far to venture and where to turn back. Still, even with the boundaries, we rub up against each other in the parks and playgrounds, the zoos, and on the public transit. We cannot escape each other: Poles, Blacks, Germans, Latinos, Jews, and American Indians—the city takes us all in and gives everyone a more or less equal shot at success and failure. My Mom tells me we are all the same and to try to love everyone. God says stay away from the projects and buy Converse high top gym shoes. They will make you run faster. I think God is paranoid, but I forgive Him. I mean, consider His past.

Chicago is a tough, raw knuckles place. Violence always lurks around the next corner, and down the alley behind our apartment. Gangs patrol the neighborhoods and hunt the lost souls who dare to cross their paths. Packs of older boys are always hassling me. In the winter they throw snowballs filled with broken glass. In the summer they take their shirts off and their muscles ripple. I see them playing basketball on the lake front courts. The baskets have chains instead of nets like the nice ones in the suburbs. The older boys play with a physical abandon I will never have. No one ever calls a foul. When a body slams into another body it sounds like a pumpkin dropped from a rooftop. One year a thousand people were murdered in the city, almost three a day. Mafia kills mafia. Drug dealers settle grudges with pawn shop guns and baseball bats. Hikers find bodies partially decomposed in the forest preserves or washed up against the banks of the Sanitary Canal, which by the way, is not sanitary at all.

I tell God you have to be so brave to grow up here. Not everyone is as immortal as Him. From the moment I became conscious, I felt all the violence the city had to offer. The evening newscasts led off each broadcast with the latest installment of mayhem. "If it bleeds it leads," was the rule. Headlines from newspapers screamed with the chilling details and the gruesome photos: Twisted bodies on sidewalks lying in haloes of blood, a crowd peering in. These were tragedies, no doubt, but they could not compare with the random murders. The couple pulled from their car and beaten to death because they got off the wrong exit at the wrong time on the Dan Ryan Expressway. The honors student shot through the heart by a stray bullet while she did her geometry homework in her bedroom—three floors above the street. No one could quite prepare for that sort of roll of dice. I always knew I could be next so I learned not to make eye contact, and to wear a protective garment of toughness and street smarts.

I picture God as clean shaven. He is of no particular ethnic group and His step is long and graceful, not the fashionable pimp roll my friends and I love to imitate. God's voice is not thunderous. Nor is it mousy. It sounds like my own, but all grown up and wise. He talks in clear, declarative sentences. He uses few adjectives. If He wrote books He would write like Hemingway. Nothing rattles Him.

I, however, am a fledgling sparrow tossed out of the nest without clear instructions. When I turned ten-years old, my mother handed me some quarters and a map, and said, "Learn the subway and bus system. Put yourself forward into the world." So I did. On Saturdays I would emerge from the subway cavern, a fiver hidden in a sock to thwart the gangs and pickpockets: Money earned from the bottle deposits I collected on a regular route of porches and stoops. I make my way to Kroch and Brentano's bookstore—the latest Hardy Boys' release on my mind. I pass the hobos and barkers on the corners conversing with their own God. I look in windows at shiny objects I will never have—fancy Lionel train sets and flashy three-speed Raleigh bicycles. I am used to this. I will catch my reflection in plate glass windows. It startles me to see my face, and my ragged clothes and uncombed hair among a sidewalk bustling with thousand-dollar suits and fashionable coiffures. I look so hungry, so young and insignificant in this big brawling city. I smell meat inside the steak braziers. I hear the doorman at the Palmer House blow his whistle for the next cab. People carry briefcases and newspapers. In the high rises, appointments begin and end. I am intoxicated. This is my city, my home and my territory, a place of definable borders and an understandable grid. I don't know what's across the lake or beyond the western horizon of prairies and rivers. I have never seen mountains. I don't know what to expect next.

God knows I never pray. The things that I want are too big, too unattainable. I want a new coat that's in style and shoes that keep my feet warm. I want to eat cheeseburgers and shoe-string french fries at every meal. I want to be play basketball above the rim like the black boys by the lake. I want an older sister. I want a pair of those X-Ray glasses advertised in the back of my Batman comic book so I can see what's beneath all those dresses and blouses. I want a four-inch switchblade. I want to be safe.

"What if something happens to my mom?" I suddenly ask Him,

while Mom and I walk down Michigan Avenue towards the train station. The shopping trip is over and my mother carries several bags. She is happy, and beautiful with her perfect carriage. She will turns heads for many years to come. "Would if she gets killed by a gangster? Or pushed off the subway platform?" Back in reality, away from the televisions and my tribe of boys, I begin to get that discombobulated feeling. I am trying hard to stay in one piece, but everything seems menacing. The el tracks block the sun and cast long shadows on the street. The businessmen are secret molesters. Strutting pigeons look predatory.

"Are you OK?" my mother asks. At the age of ten I give her the same answer I use today. "Yes, I'm fine. Everything's OK." How can I tell her that I might explode into shards of glass? Or how this city overwhelms me? She expects me to follow the unwritten code of the city: to be an unflappable urban warrior. But mostly I feel like an alien unwillingly dropped onto Earth. My body doesn't fit right. My mind fills and empties with pools of anxiety and violent imagery. My eyes won't focus on the tide of humanity that swirls around me.

We are about to descend the gum-stained stairs that lead to the Randolph Street train station when God puts His arm around me. "Look," He says, "I know how you feel. I've been around awhile and what I've learned is this: There is no other way but to be fearless. Otherwise you'll end up on one of these street corners barking at passersby and trying to get my attention.

"Trust me. Life gets better. Just hang on, at least through your twenties. Find one thing to love and run toward it with abandon, Sort of like when you look at the woman in the basement apartment. But what I'm talking about is a bit more *constructive*." I want to ask Him what he means by constructive, but He's gone. He's very busy, especially on the weekends.

After awhile the subway pops up from the tunnel and emerges into the afternoon light. With inches to spare, the train hugs and passes hundreds of three-story brick apartment buildings that are just like the ones I've lived in all my life. I see the familiar kitchen tables, shabby couches, and torn curtains, and refrigerators and stoves from the Industrial Revolution. The same laundry hanging on the back porches and the same grass-less vacant lots filled with dried weeds and car husks. Some men stand in a cluster and share a bottle. Expressionless women dream from open windows.

The subway makes one of those mystery stops between stations, and I look down and see a knot of scrawny boys playing stickball in an alley. They use their shirts for bases. They swagger and strut and scream. Next to me, my mother looks down at the same scene and smiles.

Maybe it's the little pep talk from God, or maybe I'm simply worn out from hauling around all this fear and longing. Whatever the reason, for just a moment I become one of the boys in the alley. I hold the bat in my hands. I see the ball coming. It looks as big as a pumpkin. This time I don't bail out. I hit it hard. I run faster than ever before. I touch all the bases. I am safe.

Under the Influence

In his prime my grandfather could hit the most beautiful fly balls. Behind his wood-frame house, on the long narrow lot with the rusty rabbit cages in the back and the fruit cellar where we hid from tornadoes, sat his own field of dreams. Here my grandfather was king: the empty diamond, glorious in its isolation; the clean, white chalk of the foul lines; the unattainable fence; the comforting summer smell of fresh-mown sod; and the raked dirt, ground to the fine black dust that is the life blood of eastern Iowa.

My grandparents lived their entire married life on the southwest edge of Cedar Rapids, a city in the final throes of the industrial revolution. The Quaker Oats plant and a Brer Rabbit Molasses plant emitted a grainy stench. Underneath that odor was the smell of the working class: an oily, rusty stink found in machine shops and feed stores, where men like my grandfather Chuck, with his sixth-grade education, could punch the clock and make enough to buy a house and an out-of-date Chevy pickup, then marry well and raise three lovely daughters in relative comfort.

I spent summers with them as a boy. My grandfather seemed old to me then, but he was only in his forties, just half his life lived. His days were ruled by routine. Up at 3 a.m., he'd leave for his job at the Cedar Rapids city-bus garage. Grandmother, awake with him for the moment, packed his lunch: a steel thermos of Folgers, white-bread sandwich of beef or pork, hard-boiled eggs in their shells, and a kolache or sugar-dusted piece of poppy-seed coffee cake. This was their life, year after hardworking year, until the cancers and heart disease, then the divvying-up of the backyard junk that some in my family coveted as potential antique gold (but was, alas, in the end, simply rusty junk), the eventual razing of the house that held so many memories, and the final distribution of an estate that wasn't much, but somehow held five hundred dollars for each of the grandkids.

On the baseball diamond is where I had Grandpa all to myself. While I ran to my position in the outfield, he stood at home plate, a cigar stuck in the side of his mouth, long ash ready to drop. He wore his off-work uniform of Oshkosh overalls, either a V-neck white tee or a short-sleeved shirt, and a scuffed pair of Wellingtons. On bowling league nights he slicked up in pressed slacks, western-style sports shirt, and spit-polished oxfords—all courtesy of Armstrong's in downtown Cedar Rapids, where Grandma also bought my schools clothes the week before I returned home to my mother in Chicago. Grandma always took time to indulge in her favorite lunch at the store's cafeteria: a goose-liver sandwich.

My grandparents' yard teemed with snakes—racers, greens, and garters, easy for a city boy to catch. They curled around my wrist like reptile bracelets, seeking warmth. And even when they bit, I didn't give the pain much thought. Hurts were temporary then and easily soothed with the balm of a popsicle, a bike ride, or a swim. What I do remember about those summer days is this: The world seemed large and incomprehensible. The hardwoods near the house were wild. The Cedar River, which flooded and receded along the edge of the woods, seemed as wide as the Mississippi. The furrows between cornrows were trails without end. The train trestle over the river was a trapeze without a net. Only once did I walk across it, frightened with each step, cautiously listening for whistles and watching for the cyclops of the train's light announcing a freight coming across the plains. I stopped taking such risks as I gradually learned of all the unannounced ways the world can trip you up when you are not even daring it to.

My grandfather's hitting technique began with a ritual warm-up similar to the movement of an oil derrick: Bat in his left hand, ball in his right, he would swing both arms in a circle several times, searching for the perfect timing. When bat and ball were in harmony, he would lob the ball above his head, grab the bat with both hands, and *crack*! A soaring fly—a "can of corn"— to his waiting grandson from the dark, urban streets of Chicago, a place my grandparents equated with Gomorrah. My grandfather would step back from his swing, let out a cloud of smoke from the stogie, and admire the arc of the ball that would, just for a second, disappear into the humid air.

At that perfect baseball moment, he seemed to be both there and not there. What was he thinking? His dreams and feelings he mostly kept to himself. I understood and respected this. After all, I was a shy boy who could never begin to express the tide of complex emotions that engulfed me: Separation, divorce, visitation rights, stirring hormones, and a wish to attain baseball purity. Mostly I did what I was told. Each summer, at Chicago's Union Station, my mom gave me a kiss and put me on the City of San Francisco for the train ride to Iowa to spend long weeks alone with my grandparents.

Grandpa's reverie would soon be interrupted by his certain disgust when he saw me flailing about in center field, unable to catch the easy fly ball. "Jesus Christ!" he would say, and I, the sensitive, arty boy, was temporarily ruined.

Almost every weekend during those summers Grandpa would take me along on visits to his parents' failed farm near Chelsea, where the Iowa River cuts a handsome swath, and where my Czech Aunt Herring still cooked on a wood-burning stove. It was only on those drives—after he drank several beers in the dimly lit taverns of towns like Keystone, Vining, and Elberon—that my grandfather at last let his feelings show in private, under-the-breath monologues punctuated with words I was not allowed to say. He carried on imagined conversations with relatives, both living and dead, who had done him wrong. The transformation was gradual, intensifying with each bar stop. I usually waited in the truck with a soda and a singing bladder. When I did sneak out of the pickup to peer into the dark, blue-collar bars, I saw men like my grandfather: hardworking guys sipping Old Milwaukee and Wild Turkey in the middle of the afternoon, the fog of Lucky Strike and Swisher Sweet smoke surrounding their faces in the blue glow. My grandpa would be standing at the bar, slapping down the box of dice to see if he could win his drink.

These were men who rarely strayed from their pre-ordained station. They knew the general direction their lives would go: thirty years of toil at factory or farm, a modest pension, and then all that fishing. Escape routes—St. Louis, Chicago, California even—could not compete with the pull of the familiar. Nor was escape worth the disruption. When you pushed against the mold, they believed, it always ended badly.

After a half hour or so Grandpa would come stomping out and toss me a bag of Beer Nuts, and off we would go to the next town. The change in his emotions—and his increasingly erratic driving—was startling. It was as if I no longer existed, although I sat close to him on the Chevy's bench seat. He cracked open the side vent window and lit the damp, partially chewed cigar that had been in his mouth most of the day. The summer wind blew the hot ashes back onto my bare arms, but I refused to flinch. I imagined the sharp stings as snakebites.

By now it was late evening. The truck's headlights shone on moths and mayflies, and the corn and soybean fields were ablaze with lightning bugs. Grandma would certainly be worried, looking out the front windows and getting angrier with each passing moment. The truck heaved and groaned, and when I dared to look at the speedometer, I saw we were doing eighty miles an hour. Grandpa was passing cars on steep, stomach-fluttering hills and blind curves, swerving and swearing as he steered in the general direction of Cedar Rapids. Pedal to the floor, slamming the stick shift in tandem with the abused clutch, Grandpa intensified his tirades: so-and-so was a whore, such-and-such a no good son-of-a-bitch, a bastard, or worse. For emphasis he would roll down the window and spit.

Who knows why we never crashed? Just lucky I guess. Seatbelts and air bags were nonexistent then. Our bodies were vulnerable to jagged metal, fragile windshields, and the gravelly washboard roads.

It was during those wild rides that I felt closest to Grandpa. I never complained about his driving. I kept my mouth shut, as I had been raised to do. And I dared not judge him. I didn't know at the time that drinking and driving were wrong. I knew only that I hated the same people he did, even though I had not met them. All that mattered was that they had wronged Grandpa, *my* grandpa, who hit pop flies to me in the ballpark behind the rabbit pens and the piles of rusty junk, amid the remnant prairie grasses where the snakes basked. I snuggled closer to him to show my loyalty. *See, I am your grandson. I belong to you.* Placing my head lightly against his shoulder I could smell the oil, the sweat, the Old Milwaukee.

At that moment I loved him completely—my grandfather, who could fix anything that broke down in all of Iowa, who made sauerkraut and homemade wine in the garage, who let me win at poker. I listened to him rage, and I heard every word that came spilling unfettered from the dark chambers of his heart. And I beheld him in the soothing glow from the yellow dashboard of the wobbly Chevy that would miraculously carry us back home to the rabbits and snakes, back to my grandma, and back to my roots.

Mom's Forgettable Last Days of Pleasure

There are worse moments than being told by a nurse that your dear eighty-six-year-old mother, who has dementia and resides in an assisted living facility, is sexually active.

Just kidding. There are not worse moments than when you learn that your elderly mom has been sleeping around.

Mom, who passed on two years ago, was a heart-on-the-sleeve romantic until the end, always believing that whatever exciting puppy-love magic that occurred in the first weeks of a courtship should last forever. She loved love to a fault. Three marriages and two divorces did little to change her mind.

Mom's last boyfriend was as equally demented as her. One could say it was a match made in a heavenly fog. When I was introduced to him, Mom said, "I'd like you meet my son." The boyfriend looked up from his chair with a faraway gaze as if Mom was speaking Latin. Then Mom, proudly pointing at her beau, said to me, "And I'd like you to meet...now what was your name again?"

Sure, I laugh now. Actually I laughed then, too. I mean, why not? When you spend time with someone who won't remember your visit five minutes after you have spent an entire exhausting afternoon with them, you are hardly required to remain serious, or to correct their fantasies, hallucinations or aberrant behavior. Turn that frown upside down!

So I would switch into full survival mode during those uproarious hours, downing anti-anxiety pills and popping fistfuls of Tums for my souring tummy. That's also why I didn't bother scolding Mom when I heard about her sexual proclivities. Anyway, in her condition, how much pleasure was really left to her and why should she not enjoy some forgettable sensual pleasure?

During a rare lucid moment toward the end of her life Mom did bring up the dalliances. She laughed and said, "Well, at least there is no danger of getting pregnant." Cold comfort, indeed, but comfort nonetheless, and, in those final weeks, that's really all that mattered.

When I was growing up Mom and I never discussed sex. Instead, I was forced to endure the horrors of coed sex education courtesy of the medieval Chicago Public School System. Slide shows of various diseases and disfigurements scared me celibate well into my twenties. A classmate once fainted during a particularly graphic filmstrip and flipped his desk over as he hit the floor. We made sure he never lived that moment down.

Meanwhile, Mom, newly divorced, between marriages number one and two, was on the prowl. She was dating men that came by our tiny apartment reeking of Old Spice and Vitalis. These were professional drinkers that only read racing forms and baseball box scores. Tough Chicago wise guys that would muss up my hair, bribe me with a couple of bucks to scram and go outside and play in the alley. "You're a good kid. Now get lost." (Bribery was always a way of life in the Windy City and it was good to learn the ropes early in life. Back then, with the right kind of cash discreetly palmed to the right kind of corrupt bureaucrat you could get your blind grandfather a shiny new driver's license.)

Occasionally, one of these charmers would drunk-call from a bar and beg to talk to Mom. If I answered the phone Mom would signal frantically to me that she wasn't home. Emotions of the inebriated ran from tearful regrets to angry accusations. In the background I could hear the cling of ice cubes, the crash of glasses, some mournful jukebox tune, and lots of male shouting and cursing. This led to a lifetime fear of men and the avoidance of bars.

On date nights, Mom would finally emerge from the bathroom trailing a fog of hair spray and Chanel No 5, and off she would go to the Kon Tiki Lounge or the Playboy Club. Mom was stunning with a busty centerfold body that attracted men like honey bees to blossoms. She was a powerful tigress, at the height of her sexuality and she used it well.

But now, at eighty-six, and in the final throes of mental vagueness, it was heartbreaking to connect the dots between Mom's sensual past and this diminished present. It was during those visits to the assisted living facility that I learned to ignore the sad reality of my vanishing mother and just play along, such as the time Mom suddenly decided she wanted to go back to work.

"Yes, Mom, I think you should apply for that job delivering groceries for Peapod!" But what I really thought was, *Sure, Mom, no doubt there is a plethora of openings for an eighty-six-year-old woman who routinely pours the ground Folger's in the water dispenser of their Mr. Coffee.*

Mom would then dig out a tattered sheaf of yellowed letters of recommendation from past employers, the newest one from circa 1985. She called these letters her "resumes." I browsed the letters and assured her I'd get right on it. Make a few calls. Rustle up an interview.

This made her immensely happy and hopeful. Then she tried to phone her long-deceased father with the TV remote. I didn't laugh that time.

Singing to Mom on Her Birthday

On my mother's birthday this year I will present her with the same gift she gave me: a song.

Mom loves the old standards, the ones she would sing in the bathroom every morning when she got ready for work. Those mornings in our tiny Southside Chicago apartments were filled with Mom's dramatic operatic voice combined with the odd pairing of the chemical stench of hairspray and the sweet scent of perfume.

"Georgia on My Mind" was a favorite, in no small part because her mother's name was Georgia and it was a way to honor her upbringing in rural Iowa.

"Other arms will reach out to me/Other eyes smile tenderly/Still in peaceful dreams I see/The road leads back to you..."

If it was a melancholy day, maybe a blue Monday with a busy workweek ahead, Mom might belt out Johnny Mathis' "Misty."

"Look at me/I'm as helpless as a kitten up a tree/And I feel like I'm clinging to a cloud..."

"On the Sunny Side of the Street" served as an uplifting anthem, a way perhaps of bracing herself for the long CTA commute, the four-block walk, the two buses and the El, all negotiated in high heels, dresses and nylons, no doubt enduring the catcalls of construction workers and leering commuters. Did I mention Mom was drop dead gorgeous?

"Grab your coat and get your hat/Leave your worry on the doorstep/Just direct your feet/To the sunny side of the street..."

Those daily treks in the 1960s and 70s, no matter what weather conditions confronted her—and there is no worse weather than Chicago's—were to low-level clerical jobs in hospitals and insurance companies. I don't think Mom ever made more than six dollars an hour.

I want to let you know that for a time my mother was a single mom, that she worked so hard to provide for me, and that on Saturday she often slept long into the afternoon on the fold-out couch in the living room that served as her bed. She was exhausted.

I also think it's important to say that although we may have been poor by today's standards, I never felt impoverished. Our neighborhood was a level playing field of lower to middle class working families, all residing in the same ancient, three-story apartment buildings that defined the skyline of our urban territory.

Like so many of those families, we did not have a car because, well, in addition to the expense, we didn't need one. Chicago's mass transit system served us well, and unlike today, when overly-anxious parents double as armed chauffeurs, I simply walked to school, each morning leaving the apartment and joining the confluence of kids all headed in the same direction.

Sympathy or pity are not my reasons for describing our life. My real purpose is to flesh out an existence that at first glance might seem quite ordinary. But over time I have learned there are no ordinary lives. What Mom did in caring for me, in filling our home with love and music, and instilling solid values that have sustained me well into my sixties, was nothing short of heroic. The old saw that children raised by single parents are disadvantaged and will not do as well as kids from "intact" two-parent families is an unfair stereotype that badly needs amending. Each situation is unique. The story of any life can be told in one chapter: how we survive all that the years throw at us. The addendum to that chapter is that there is no rhyme or reason to any of it.

I might well have benefitted from the nurturing of two functional parents, but that's a crapshoot, too. The special bond that developed with my mom might not have occurred if Dad had stuck around. Earlier than other children, perhaps, I learned survival techniques, learned to rely on my wits and my own instincts and to never ever disappoint Mom.
******

Mom passed away almost three years ago. Her ashes sit in a box upon the old black Sears trunk in my office she bought me when I left Chicago for good in 1973. This year, on the morning of her birthday, a day in which her memory will be especially vivid, I will pick up my old guitar and sing an inadequate version of "What A Wonderful World," that ballad of promise and renewal that Louis Armstrong made famous.

"The colors of the rainbow so pretty in the sky/Are also on the faces of people going by/I see friends shaking hands saying how do you do/They're really saying I love you..."

And, as with every year since she has passed, when I close my eyes, I will smell the hairspray and perfume, and hear Mom singing harmony, her voice as clear and confident as ever, as if she is still here, surrounding me with her everlasting love.

Searching for A Way Home

Shortly after our latest war in the Middle East began, I waited in line at my local post office. Ahead of me stood a man holding a large parcel. He wore a scraggly beard, un-styled hair, and faded Levis. He was around fifty. One of my numerous faults is to label people without sufficient information. The kid with the hat turned backwards and the baggy pants dragging on the ground *must* be gang-affiliated when, in fact, he is on his way to an advanced physics class. The African-American men approaching me on the sidewalk *are* threatening gangsters, but they ignore me, instead lost in conversation about their residencies at the hospital. The man with the southern drawl has got to be a white supremacist. He runs a mission for minorities.

Maybe it was the beard—a rarity in this farm town, except for the Amish who live a few towns over—but I decided the man with the box at the post office was a former Vietnam demonstrator and probably a current anti-war protestor. I even went so far in my imagination to think that he had, like me, lived at one time in the Northwest. Maybe we had mutual acquaintances and lived in the same dead-end mill towns. My characterization of this man made me feel better. Virtually no dissent existed in this farm town, although in the nearby university town pro-peace rallies occurred daily. Yellow ribbons were tied around ancient sycamores and oaks, and flags flapped loudly from minivans. The man's presence, his relaxed dress, chipped away a bit of the loneliness I'd been experiencing.

"How is your son doing?" the clerk asked the man. "Is he still on the U.S.S. Abraham Lincoln?"

"Yes. He's fine, anxious to get home. His outfit just set a record for the longest deployment in the history of the Navy. They're just doing circles in the Gulf of Oman."

The postal clerk and the father of the sailor talk for another ten minutes about families, local gossip, and the weather. I wait patiently in line. In a small town you learn to wait.

When the father of the sailor finishes, he turns around and looks me over. There is no recognition. For the hundredth time I feel that odd, lonesome feeling of an alien or an intruder. "I hope your son comes back safely," I tell him. He thanks me and I move to the front of the line feeling like the outsider that I am.

After three years in the corn belt I am restless. To stay busy I've kept up my volunteerism at the nursing home, but I've taken to passing on the simplest of other good citizenship duties: donating blood and voting. In my weak defense, the Red Cross phlebotomists are brutal with the needle (I'm always left with bruises), and most local candidates run unopposed on the local Republican ticket. I don't blame the town for my restlessness. A place is neutral and, as I've already shown, we mostly live in our minds anyway. Topography is also not a factor. Flat land doesn't annoy me particularly. Forest trails are just a ten-minute drive away and a river keeps the herons and ducks flying overhead. If you deduct the speeding tickets and DUIs, crime is nonexistent. You can walk anywhere at any hour of the night. People are generally friendly and welcoming. The mythical town of "Pleasantville" has nothing on this white-fenced, wood-framed-housed slice of Americana. But like the James McMurtry song, "I'm not from here, I just live here."

I keep my bags packed and my exit doors unobstructed. Nine states fill my life resume, destinations like Bark River in Michigan's Upper Peninsula, where I raked barley in fields surrounded by hardwoods. Astoria, Oregon, where I planted trees on treacherous hills in relentless rain. Tucson's skid row, where I drove an ice cream truck and lived across the street from the blood donation center. Northern California, where I made tofu for more than two years and was paid $136 a week. Money was never the goal. The objective was romantic, if not altogether vague. Once I had a taste of motion and the inspiration of landscape, I was hooked.

I've hung my hat in log cabins, unheated trailers, leaky tents, sleeping bags under the stars, ranch houses, apartments, highway culverts, strangers' basements, and friends' couches. But before long, in every place I've dared to call home, I always began dreaming about the next new destination. I still scour maps, looking for the most obscure passage, or the longest stretch on the atlas without a road. Where can I go to initiate that addictive sense of magic and wonder—that delicious two-month long disorientation and discovery period—when one finds the best two-egg breakfast, the friendliest waitresses; the meanest dogs, the loveliest houses, and the best-stocked libraries? Where is that undiscovered American town, that slice of authenticity, a place that doesn't yet know all the slick ways to pretend to be unpretentious?

At first I wore my restlessness like a badge. Jack Kerouac's *On the Road* was my bible. "Now, Sal," says crazy Dean Moriarty, "we're leaving everything behind us and entering a new and unknown phase of things. All the years and troubles and kicks—and now this! So we can safely think of nothing else and just go on ahead with our faces stuck out like this, you see, and understand the world as, really and genuinely speaking, other Americans haven't done before us...."

But I am not a fictional character.

Transience comes with consequences. You can never really be a "local," even in the youthful West where a two-year residency elevates you to "native" status. The real community—the enviable, agrarian one that revolves around life and death, planting and harvest, cemeteries, granges, church potlucks—will always be out of reach. Now that I am nearing sixty, there are not even the required years remaining to sink roots deep enough into this black Midwest soil. Even if I endure a twenty- to thirty-year residency in this close-knit town, I will always be viewed as a newcomer or, at most, the husband of my wife, who was born in the area and has most of her relatives here.

I accepted that status when I came here, thinking I could stave off the inevitable migrating ache in my heart. In the dark winter and the humid summer months I can manage. But when the redbuds bloom in the spring and the snow geese fly over in the fall, I begin to plot my escape. Nights are the worst. Recurring dreams about tearful reunions with old friends jolt me awake. I walk around the dark house in an attempt to come back to the present, but then a momentary sensory trigger stops me in my tracks. How is it, from a living room in the Midwest twenty years after the fact, that I can suddenly smell juniper berries or feel the exhilaration of a moon rising or remember a dream about black bears? Whatever walls exist between the past and present disintegrate, and I would pay dearly to control that uncontrollable urge to cut and run. But run where?

I write these words and yet they are lies. For a place will grow on if you let it, if you begin to live a life outside yourself. I keep thinking back to August of 2000, three months after my wife and I had moved back to Illinois. I won't go through all the details of my father-in-law's struggle with cancer. Most of us know how horrible cancer is. Melanoma is particularly evil. So check your moles, wear sunscreen, and pray.

The long week's vigil at the hospital has ended. Cancer has won. Howard has just passed away and we stand there surrounding his still body in the hospital bed: Betty, his wife of fifty-five years, his two daughters, his son, and me, the newest member of the family. We have cried, held hands, and prayed over his body, we have allowed the doctor to come in and pronounce him dead, and we have called the undertaker. Phone calls and arrangements have to be made. I stand across from Betty, trying not to be noticed, and let the family have their space to mourn. But she finds me, looks me in the eye, points a finger at me, and says, "And you, you will write and deliver the eulogy."

It was an offer I could not refuse, a request from which I could not run.

So on a hot humid August morning in DeLand, Illinois, another American town on life support—population either 450 or 350 depending on which sign you read when you enter the town—I put on Howard's clothes, his light blue summer blazer bought at Delbert's, an Amish store over in Arthur. I tied his flowered tie around my neck, and buttoned up his short-sleeve dress shirt. All of the clothes were too big, too symbolic, and I knew there was no way I would ever grow into them. I stood at the altar in the small Methodist church, where most Sundays the congregation numbers twenty, almost all of the congregation is over seventy and widowed, and where in three more years the church would close.

I stood there as Betty asked me to, in front of people connected at the roots like the oldest stand of oaks in the county: These people had known everything about Howard and each other for more than half a century. I stood, a newcomer, trying to sum up in a few pages what this man's passing meant. In the front pew Betty, daughters Beth and Jan, and son Steven, still farms the home place. They all listened. Here's part of what I said:

"Howard's life spanned a period of time covering most of the history of Illinois agriculture—plow horse to thresher to combine. He was an innovator and took pride in his crops. He served on so many boards and committees, from the Deland-Weldon School Board to Goosecreek Township Drainage Commission, and every board in between. He served because that is what you do with life—you immerse yourself in it, and for Howard, such a social and talkative man, the boards were very rewarding. He lived through world wars, watched the freeways unfurl across the country, and through it all he stayed in this community he loved so dearly.

"A thousand people from Howard's generation—the greatest generation, no question about it—die each day in this country. They are the reservoir for our wisdom. They are our bedrock, our sustenance. With them go not only the history of farm and soil, but also the ability to mend fences and the art of compromise. And when the last of this generation passes, who will tell us stories?

"Like this story he told to his daughter Jan recently about the time his parents, Ola and Parley, took him and his three little sisters to DeWitt for their diphtheria shots. Howard could see the children ahead of him in line receiving those dreadful shots, crying out in pain, and running back to their parents dribbling tears the whole way. Closer and closer the line crept forward to where the nurse was waiting with the long needle. At the last possible moment, when no one was looking, he grabbed his arm, gave out a war cry of pain, and ran out the door. His poor sisters had to actually receive their shots, and their arms stung like wasps' bites. On the way home he confessed his mischief to his parents, but they didn't turn the car around. The shame of the confession was punishment enough.

"Or the time long ago when he and his best friend Halsey ate an entire quart of ice cream in one fabulous afternoon. Here are his own words: 'Hot afternoons between chores we'd go to the People's Cafe in Farmer City, sit up at the counter and order a quart. Hard as a rock it was, kept in dry ice. They cut it with a cleaver into two square chunks, just like it was steak.

"'We were teen-age boys and because of that we wouldn't stop eating until we finished it in one sitting. Now that was good. Now that was all right.'

"Who will tell us these stories?

"The time in 1939 when he and Lyle Resser and Paul Longenbaugh drove across the country to Washington, D.C. in the car Howard borrowed from his dad. This was historic—his very first long-distance driving trip—and they lunched and camped in fields along the way. But the best part of the story, according to Howard, was their thriftiness. In a week's time, he proudly remembered, they each spent $9.32.

"So many stories we still want to hear. Stories we need to hear.

"Howard, like all the men and women of this generation knew the important things. He knew that the only remaining store in DeWitt once sold Buffalo Chewing Tobacco. He knew the exact date electricity came to his family's Deland farm, 1945, nine years after they moved there. He could always find the remains of the schools that have been long torn down.

"He knew to use gun grease on his bird feeder stand to keep the squirrels at bay. But you know how it is with squirrels; you can only fool them for so long. And, as his son, Steven recounted to me, Howard knew in great detail how to kill chinch bugs with logs, post holes, and an unhealthy dose of creosote.

"And there was Howard's pride of conduct. He knew how to carry himself forward into this world, and his courage carried him to the next. Betty said one of the qualities she admired most about her husband was his devotion to his parents in their illnesses and in their aging. Here, then, is perhaps the best way to be beloved.

"His mother Ola taught him the importance of knowing how to spell, to use a good vocabulary, and to speak well. Swearing is sloppy and unacceptable. Cynicism is a weakness. Wallowing in self-pity just wasted precious time. The bright light of life was where Howard wanted to bask, not the dark recesses of gloom. Even when he was dying he was searching for light, always searching for a way to make *us*, the healthy ones, feel more comfortable.

"To be called beloved you have to be smart. And Howard was smart enough to marry well; to join forces fifty-five years ago with Betty Jean, who he sometimes called his "navigator." She guided them across this great country on their many trips, and she navigated him gracefully though his illness to his final gentle breath. They made a warm place within their home for siblings, cousins, nieces, nephews, grandkids, and six years ago they took in new son-in-law, even, as Howard said with a wink in my direction, if he was a Democrat. We gravitated toward Howard's light and he folded us all up in his big arms.

"When he retired to Monticello from the farm, Howard set up what became known as Command Central, his big, brown leather chair from where he ran everything—phones, remotes, the unraveling of the morning paper, the evening news, trip planning, calling friends and family, and always telling more stories. He stayed active in farming even after retiring, helping Steve with planting and harvest. There was Rotary on Wednesdays, weekly trips to the elevator to participate in the finely-honed art of loafing, drives through the countryside to check on crops and reminisce, And each afternoon around 3 p.m. he'd head over to Hardee's to attend that day's official session of the Liar's Club.

"In 79 years, such a rich life of accomplishment and family and duty, but still he wanted more and, more than ever, we wanted more…of Howard.

"Howard, my dear friend, you are beloved by all of us, and you will always be with us, in this church, in our homes, in these bountiful fields of grain, among the gathering geese, across the big prairie sunsets and moon rises, in these precious communities of faith and flag. You are here with us today, your roots sink deep into the rich fertile soil of our grieving hearts. "

—————

Then we carried the coffin out to the country cemetery. The cherrywood coffin was heavy. Six of us sweating out the humidity, carried Howard down the church steps for the last time. I was the only man under the age of fifty to be a pallbearer.

Halsey, Howard's best friend, a man of few words came up to me as I was leaving and said, "Nice words." That's all he said. It was enough.

During that first harvest with Howard gone, I saw the ramifications of what his passing meant. Riding with Steven in the combine cutting corn, I noticed he was consulting a worn pocket notebook with tiny perfect script: odd numbers and fragments of sentences with underlinings and scratchouts. These were Howard's combine settings for corn and soybeans. And there in the golden September harvest light, the words and numbers were fading before his eyes.

"Do you want me to copy all those notes down on computer, Steve?" I asked.

"No, this is fine. This is OK."

I am trying to be at home in this new place. I am trying not to live another lie. Close the back doors. Seal the escape hatches. Try to be like my father-in-law. Drop the pose. Be an asset. Contribute to community.

I run each afternoon through the city cemetery, past Veteran's Hill, past century-old oaks and headstones, past the fresh graves with the fresh flowers scattered on the mounds. Slowly the names are becoming more familiar. The obituaries in the weekly newspaper have meaning now. Vast flat fields reveal themselves to be a way of measuring worth and value. Slowly, in the time I am blessed to have remaining, this place will someday be home.

One of the headstones reads: "Life is temporary, Love is forever."

This is what endures.

Stephen J. Lyons is the author of five books of essays and journalism: *Landscape of the Heart: Writings on Daughters and Journeys*, *A View from the Inland Northwest*, *The 1,000-Year Flood: Destruction, Loss, Rescue, and Redemption along the Mississippi River*, *Going Driftless: Life Lessons from the Heartland for Unraveling Times*, and *West of East* (Finishing Line Press).

Stephen is a two-time recipient of a fellowship in prose writing from the Illinois Arts Council and has published articles, reviews, essays, and poems in numerous publications, including *Wall Street Journal*, *Washington Post*, *Salon*, *The Independent*, *Toronto Globe & Mail*, *Manoa*, *Newsweek*, *The Sun*, *Chicago Tribune*, *Funny Times*, *Witness*, and *High Country News*. His work has been featured in fifteen anthologies alongside such noted writers as Barry Lopez, Peter Matthiessen, Edward Abbey, Barbara Kingsolver, Anna Quindlen, Dave Barry, and Louise Erdrich.

Stephen is a native of the South Side of Chicago and a product of that city's legendary public education system. After living for thirty years in the West, he now resides in a small farming town in central Illinois that often smells of soy. He's been employed in nine different states as a tree planter, daffodil picker, dude ranch cook, a model for Porsche, ice cream vendor, magazine editor, phone solicitor, newspaper reporter, tofu maker, grain truck driver, assistant dairy herdsman, and agricultural extension editor. He once worked for a week in Colorado pulling nails out of two-by-fours, and for one twelve-hour day picking hops in southern Oregon until he was fired for claiming the foreman had bad karma.